Praise for *Brightly Shining*

'An emotionally packed little gem'
—*New York Times Book Review*

'A winning holiday tale with just the right proportions of hardship and hope' —***Wall Street Journal***

'This tender novel does exactly what it promises: shines brightly despite the darkness'
—***Oprah Daily*, Best Books of 2024**

'The perfect literary stocking stuffer' —***Air Mail***

'This moving tale, with not a single wasted word, asks how we keep going when hope fades and life's burdens become too much to bear' —***Booklist***

'A dazzling contemporary fable of hardship and grit about two sisters who refuse to lose hope. Curl up with it for instant hygge and a warming of the heart'
—**Lily King, author of *Writers & Lovers***

INGVILD RISHØI was born and raised in Oslo. She has published several collections of stories in Norway, and her debut novel *Brightly Shining*, originally titled *Stargate*, was released in Norway in 2021. It is published or forthcoming in thirty territories and is being adapted for film. Rishøi is one of Norway's most revered literary voices and her latest work, *Winter Stories*, will be published for Christmas 2025.

CAROLINE WAIGHT is a literary translator working from Danish, German and Norwegian. She has been a finalist for the PEN Translation Prize and the Warwick Prize for Women in Translation. She lives near London.

Brightly Shining

INGVILD RISHØI

**Translated from the Norwegian
by Caroline Waight**

Grove Press UK

First published in the United Kingdom in 2024 by Grove Press UK,
an imprint of Grove Atlantic
First published in the United States of America in 2024 by Grove Atlantic
This paperback edition first published in the United Kingdom in 2025 by
Grove Press UK, an imprint of Grove Atlantic

Copyright © Ingvild Rishøi, 2024
English translation © Caroline Waight, 2024

The moral right of Ingvild Rishøi to be identified as the author of this work
has been asserted by her in accordance with the Copyright, Designs and
Patents Act of 1988.

All rights reserved. No part of this publication may be reproduced, stored
in a retrieval system, or transmitted in any form or by any means, electronic,
mechanical, photocopying, recording, or otherwise, without the prior permission
of both the copyright owner and the above publisher of the book.

This novel is entirely a work of fiction. The names, characters and incidents
portrayed in it are the work of the author's imagination. Any resemblance to actual
persons, living or dead, events or localities, is entirely coincidental.

No part of this book may be used in any manner in the learning, training or
development of generative artificial intelligence technologies (including but not
limited to machine learning models and large language models (LLMs)), whether
by data scraping, data mining or use in any way to create or form a part of data
sets or in any other way.

This translation has been published with the financial support of NORLA.

1 3 5 7 9 8 6 4 2

A CIP record for this book is available from the British Library.

Paperback ISBN 978 1 80471 075 3
E-book ISBN 978 1 80471 074 6

Printed and bound by CPI (UK) Ltd, Croydon CR0 4YY

Grove Press UK
Ormond House
26–27 Boswell Street
London
WC1N 3JZ

www.atlantic-books.co.uk

Product safety EU representative: Authorised Rep Compliance Ltd.,
Ground Floor, 71 Lower Baggot Street, Dublin, D02 P593, Ireland.
www.arccompliance.com

Brightly Shining

Sometimes I think about Tøyen. It's then I see Tøyen quite clearly.

People carrying shopping bags out of the supermarket and pushing buggies through the snow, running to school with bags thumping, and the caretaker standing by the gate at break time, smoking. Then the snow melts, and the Christmas trees lie brown outside the blocks of flats, and then the lawns turn green and full of dandelions, and so it goes on, people walking steadily and staggering and walking steadily again, babies being born and old folk dying, and at break time the caretaker leans against the pillar by the gate, blowing smoke towards the sky.

It's then he thinks of me. He understood it all, I see that now. He gazes up above the rooftops and remembers everything.

"Standing out here, are we?" the caretaker said.

He took up position at his pillar, taking a packet of cigarettes out of his pocket. And I stood where I always stood, I answered as I always used to answer.

"Yes," I said.

"You know that's not allowed?" the caretaker said.

I gave him the reply I'd learned from Dad.

"Rules are made to be broken."

It was snowing a little. Behind us, someone was shouting *eeny meeny miny moe!* The caretaker stooped and lit his cigarette. Then we picked up our conversation.

"You know that's not allowed?" I said.

"Rules are made to be broken," the caretaker said. "Did you give away all your food again?"

I nodded. The squirrel had already been, Tøyen's only squirrel and its finest. It knew when break time was, and then it came. The caretaker held the cigarette between his lips and took his packed lunch out of his pocket. He opened the foil, split the börek in two, and passed me one still-steaming half. His wife was very good at wrapping.

"It's the circle of life," the caretaker said. "You give to the squirrel, I give to you."

"What's the circle of life?" I said.

"Philosophy," said the caretaker. "Here I am a caretaker, you know. But in my home country I was a great thinker."

He turned and blew the smoke away from me.

"That's the good thing about being an immigrant," he said. "You can always tell people what you were in your home country."

"But you're pulling their legs?" I said.

"Never," he said. "Well, actually, in my home country I was one of the country's greatest leg-pullers. I won a competition. The National Leg-Pulling Championships."

"Gosh," I said.

"Anyway," he said. "Have you seen that flyer over there?"

And he pointed with the cigarette between his fingers.

Wanted: Christmas Tree Seller, it read. *You Are: Conscientious. Responsible. Outdoorsy.*

It was taped to a lamppost. At the bottom were strips of paper with a telephone number.

"Might be of interest?" the caretaker said.

"I don't think ten-year-olds can get jobs, can they?" I said.

"It's not you I was thinking of," the caretaker said.

He went up to the lamppost and tore off one of the strips, and came back and put it in my hand.

"Show that to your dad," he said.

Snowflakes were melting around the bit of paper in my palm.

"And if he does apply for the job, tell him to say he knows Alfred," said the caretaker. "He's the one who delivers the Christmas trees for them."

"But is that true?" I said.

"True enough," the caretaker said. "I know Alfred, you know me, and your dad knows you. That's the circle of life."

I nodded.

"While we're at it," said the caretaker, "you might as well take the whole thing."

And he went back over, picked off the tape, and rolled the flyer into a scroll.

"It's not allowed, putting up flyers here," he said.

"But what if somebody else wants to apply for the job?" I said.

The caretaker tucked the scroll into my jacket pocket. Snowflakes were landing on his small woolly hat.

"Exactly," he said. "You're looking at a great thinker here."

When I got home, Dad was sitting at the kitchen table. Looking up, he shielded his eyes with his hand.

"Is that the sun coming up?" he said. "Where are my sunglasses?"

He smiled, I smiled too. Then he stopped smiling.

"Come and sit here for a minute," he said.

He rubbed his forehead. But I didn't want him to start up. *This is no way for kids to live*, he says, *tarmac and all this shit*, and afterwards he says, *but you're not stupid, you two, nobody can say that, and you've had good times too, remember the tent that summer? Remember the cabin that winter?* and I answer yes and no and yes, but I didn't want him to start up again, so I unrolled the flyer and put it on the table.

"Christmas Tree Seller," said Dad.

The flyer rolled up by itself. I rolled it flat again and held it down. He looked up.

"But a Christmas tree seller," he said. "That's a job for country bumpkins, Ronja."

"But anything is better than nothing," I said.

Then he looked again at the flyer. And suddenly he got up and went over to the counter and picked up the kettle. Turning on the tap, he said, "You're not stupid, you know. You never have been."

He filled the kettle. I love it when he drinks coffee. And when he grabs a pair of joggers and puts them on, and when he looks out of the window and starts to pace about, I love it. I remember all the jobs that Dad has had. The best one was the bakery, when he brought home giant cinnamon rolls, and I could eat them the next day at school, where the others peered into my lunch box like, *no way*, and Musse said, *man, you're always lucky*, and Stella said, *you know that's not allowed?* and Musse said, *chill out, Stella, everybody else's packed lunch is full of sugar anyway*. But the supermarket one was good too, and the one where he washed the trams, and the others used to say, *your dad works at the supermarket, right, can you get me a discount on chocolate milk? Your dad washes the trams, right, can you ask him not to wash off the bits my brother tagged?* The only one that wasn't good was when he was a poet and wrote about how thought was an eel in a trap and sold the poems outside 7-Eleven, I didn't love that one, but I love it when the kettle starts to hiss, and that's all it takes. *You two dream too much*, Melissa likes to say, *if dreaming was a job we could move right now to the fancy streets in Holmenkollen.*

The water bubbled. Dad picked up the kettle. And my head was already full of dreams. Because I knew where the Christmas tree market was, and I was thinking I could run over there straight after school, and Dad would be walking around among the trees in his woolly jumper, and I could stand over by the petrol station and watch him smile at the customers and put their money in a fat wallet. Then he'd get paid, and for Christmas we could give Melissa, I don't know, something she wanted, and Dad would buy it and come home and beckon me into the bathroom and whisper, *look, this is the sort of thing sixteen-year-olds are into, right?* I thought it might be Dad who delivered the Christmas tree to school as well. I knew exactly what it would be like—Meron would lean against the window and yell, *the Christmas tree is coming! The Christmas tree is coming! Look, it's Ronja's dad, yeah!* And the teacher says *sit, sit, stay in your seats*, but everybody runs over to the window, yeah, then everybody runs over to the window, and downstairs we see the head teacher crossing the playground to meet Dad. She's got her arms clutched around her wool coat. Then she points towards the gym. Her knitted belt is flapping in the wind, and Dad is smiling his big smile, and Dad hauls the tree through the school gate, and everyone in class yells *wow*. That's what I dreamed.

Dad stood looking out of the window. It was still snowing. He held the mug to his chest. Our kitchen was so empty.

"Maybe we can have a Christmas tree this year, then," I said.

"What?" said Dad.

"If you're a Christmas tree seller," I said. "Then can we have a Christmas tree?"

"Of course," said Dad, turning to face me. "My Robber's Daughter. You reckon employees get a discount?"

"Yeah, definitely," I said.

"Or even a free tree, maybe?" Dad said, and I nodded, because I did think so.

"My Robber's Daughter," Dad liked to call me. "You are my Robber's Daughter and my Treasure Chest and my Rainy-Day Fund."

He liked to call us Star and Moon and Macaroni and Caramel. He called us Ronja the Robber's Daughter and Melissa Moonlight, he walked in through the door and said, "Where's my Robber's Daughter and my Moonlight?"

"Here," we'd say. "We're just sitting here eating Frosties."

"But do you think he'll get the job?" I said.

I was lying in the crook of Melissa's shoulder. The beams of cars' headlamps moved across the ceiling.

"No," Melissa said. "Of course not."

She picked at the tear in the wallpaper.

"But if he does. You'd want us to have a Christmas tree too, right?"

Melissa stopped picking.

"I mean, you think a Christmas tree would be nice, don't you?"

"Ronja," she said. "A Christmas tree costs maybe six hundred kroner."

Outside, a car honked its horn. Somebody shouted, *oy, watch where you're going!*

"It's icy," Melissa said. "It's that freezing rain."

"But Melissa," I said. "Don't you think we'd get a discount on Christmas trees if he was working there?"

"But he isn't working there," she said. "In case you'd forgotten. Try to think about something else."

But I didn't want to think about anything else. I screwed up my eyes until I had a head full of Christmas trees.

"But *if*," I said. "It will help if he says hi from Alfred, don't you think?"

"Sure," Melissa said. "Can we sleep now?"

"But if he says hi from Alfred and if he gets the job and if there's an employee discount," I said. "I'm just wondering: would you want to decorate the tree straightaway? Or would you wait until Christmas?"

Melissa looked at me.

"I don't want to dream like that," she said.

"Just a little bit?" I said. "Just one teeny tiny dream?"

"Jesus fuck," she said, but she'd given in, I could tell, the way she looked up at the ceiling and her body relaxed. She took my hand under the duvet.

"Sure," she said. "If we get a Christmas tree."

"Yeah," I said.

"Then we'll put it in the living room," she said.

"But can you say that it's a cabin?" I said.

She looked at me. "Okay, the thing I don't get is that you know exactly what I'm supposed to say," she said. "Why can't you just tell the story yourself?"

"Sweet Caramel?" I said.

She shut her eyes. "Okay," she said. "We are now in a cabin. Deep, deep in the woods. With a fireplace, the whole shebang. And then, on Christmas Eve itself, in the morning, when it's dark."

"Yes?" I said.

"We go into the living room and light the candles on the tree," she said. "And the way they glow is just . . . incredible."

"Yeah," I said. "Like in 'The Little Match Girl.'"

"Don't think about that," Melissa said. "That's the saddest story ever."

"But remember the tree?" I said. "Don't you remember the tree she's looking at?"

"She's hallucinating," Melissa said. "Don't think about that. The girl dies at the end, you know."

"She doesn't die," I said. "She goes to her grandma."

Melissa took a breath and shook her head, but then she put her face to mine, her mouth right up close to my ear, and she spoke softly, about Christmas decorations and log fires and smoke that rose towards the sky, deep, deep within the woods.

Then you'll have to find the path. You'll know it when you do, because there'll be a sort of portal in the woods—there's snow on the trees, and they stoop over you as you begin to walk. And you begin to walk. It's easy, because the snow along the path is trodden firm. Then there's a clearing, and you see the lake, flat and white, and the hill where the fox has its den, and at the top you see the fence, and you'll follow that, and you know what you'll see then.

"Girls," Dad called to us. "I got the job."

It was the next day, after school. We were sitting at the table. My mouth was full of Frosties and milk. Dad was standing in the kitchen doorway. He smiled and dropped his leather jacket on the floor, then he came up to us and tossed some sheets of paper on the table.

"I got it," he said.

Melissa put her spoon down in her bowl.

"Congratulations," she said. "When do you start?"

"Tomorrow," Dad said.

"You should set an alarm, then," Melissa said.

"This job is perfect," Dad said. "It starts at ten."

"Miracles do happen," the caretaker used to say. "Sometimes there just isn't any other way out, and that's when a miracle happens."

When we got home the next day, he was gone. We sat at the kitchen table again, we ate Frosties again. It was dark outside, and Dad wasn't there.

"Do you believe he's at work?" I said.

"I don't believe anything," Melissa said. "Believing's for the mosque."

"But if you had to guess? Where would you guess he is?"

Then the front door opened, I jumped, and Dad cried, "Hello there, oof, it's nice and warm in here!"

Melissa stopped eating. Dad kicked off his shoes and came into the kitchen. He was wearing his woolly jumper, and it was covered in needles. He put his mittens to dry on the radiator. He'd just been at work, then he'd come home again. He was just opening the cupboard and throwing a whole packet of spaghetti into a saucepan. Then he went out into the hall and rummaged through the drawers and said he needed more mittens.

"You have no idea how wet fir trees get in this weather," he said. "Unless you work with them, you've got no idea."

Afterwards he sat down at the table and began to talk. He'd just been at work then come straight home, and I knew what Melissa was thinking, it won't go on like this, she thought, and yet it did.

It went on. Every day we ate spaghetti. Every day he talked about the job. He said the boss was a little dictator and the firs were fat and heavy as pigs, but he smiled, he squirted ketchup onto the spaghetti, he said his neck and fingers and backside were sore, and Melissa twirled spaghetti round her fork and kept her eyes down, but I stared at Dad, because miracles do happen. They have happened. He talked about November in the Christmas tree industry and about chopping and loading and nursing homes, which have to have two or three Christmas trees one after another, because that's how long Christmas lasts at a nursing home, *and the elderly can't be doing with plastic*, Dad said, *old folk deserve the smell of fir*. He talked while he washed the saucepan. He talked while I did homework. And while I brushed my teeth, he sat on the toilet lid and talked about the tree farm at Enebakk and the tree farm at Moss and what kind of tree we'd buy, a fjord spruce, if we were lucky and there were any left by the time he'd been paid, and then at last he sat on the edge of the bed and undid the tangles in my hair and talked about silver firs and ordinary firs and Sitka firs and lots of other firs I can't remember anymore.

And Monday came and Tuesday and Wednesday, and he talked about the cabin we would buy if he could just get a regular job. Thursday came and Friday, and he talked about the path and the fence and how we'd sit out on the doorstep and look up at the Big Dipper, and then it was Saturday, and there was a knock at the door.

Dad let go of my hair and stood up off the bed. But ours wasn't really a flat where people came knocking. Only Aronsen came knocking round our flat, *I'm calling the police*, he'd say, but he never called the police. But before, when I was little, I thought he would. He'd be standing there in his dressing gown and I'd be clutching Dad's legs and crying, *don't call, don't call*, until Aronsen looked down and said, *hush now, I'm not calling anybody, I'm just trying to get this into your dad's head.*

Dad went into the hall. I heard him answer. I found a corner of the duvet cover and bit it.

"Hello, there," said Dad.

"How's it going?" said a lady. "Haven't seen you in a while."

It was Sonja.

"I was just wondering," she said. "Nothing's happened, has it?"

Yes, that was Sonja. I'd met her at the Friend at Hand and had seen her lean towards Dad across the table. And I hated the Friend at Hand. *They should call that place the Enemy at Hand*, Melissa liked to say. *That place ought to be closed down.* I'd met her at Stargate also, Stargate which I also hated, the stars above the door and the darkness inside and how their table was way over in the corner, so you had to walk through all the darkness just to find him, and that's where Sonja used to sit and smile. She'd sat on our sofa too, and talked to me, and I hated the smell of her breath, and now she was standing in the corridor outside, asking Dad whether anything had happened. *Yeah, a few of us were wondering*, Sonja said, *we've got to look out for each other, you know, no one else is going to.*

"Nothing's happened," Dad said. "I've just been working."

"Oh right, great," Sonja said. "But we'll be seeing you back there sometime soon, won't we?"

I chewed and bit the flap of duvet cover.

"We'll see," said Dad. "I have to get up early these days, you know."

Then they talked too quietly. But after a minute I heard Sonja.

"Ten o'clock?" she said. "But that means you can have a lie-in, doesn't it?"

"Yeah, sort of," said Dad.

"You could drop by tonight, then." Sonja said.

I stopped chewing, the air whistling in my ears. Dad cleared his throat in the hall. The neighbour flushed the toilet.

"Not tonight," said Dad. "I'm taking it easy."

I felt dizzy. Sonja was saying something in the hall, but I didn't hear what, because my heart was thudding so loudly. I had to lie on my front and squash it flat so it wouldn't thud itself to smithereens.

He went on sitting on the edge of my bed. Every night he sat there. He undid my tangles and talked to me about the deepest forests and the narrowest paths. He spoke the names as well, *Forest of the Finns*, he said, *Fathom Isle* and *Femund Field, but now it's getting late, and my Little Rainy-Day Fund's got to sleep.*

Then one day we came home, Melissa and me. We kicked off our shoes and went into the kitchen and opened the fridge and it was full.

"Hey!" I said. "Look!"

"Okay," Melissa said.

I looked at her.

"But look," I said. "It's the Christmas food!"

"Yup," she said. "Let's eat, then."

She opened the bread bin and cut up lots of bread. She fetched plates and cheese and ham and liver-pâté spread. There were elves and sleighs on the milk carton. She poured squash and milk and fizzy Christmas drinks into different glasses. She smeared thick layers of butter, and we ate four slices each, but she didn't look at me.

We were drinking Christmas fizz when Dad came. He was holding more bags, which he set on the kitchen countertop, and smiled.

"Where did you get the money for this food?" Melissa said.

"What?" said Dad. "Hello to you too."

"Hello," Melissa said. "Where did you get the money for this food?"

"I asked for an advance," Dad said, and he leaned over the bags and took out a packet of Nesquik.

"Here," he said, holding it out. "Isn't this the one you like?"

I nodded.

"And you got it?" Melissa said. "An advance?"

"That Eriksen's a decent chap," said Dad, opening the cabinet. "So he said yes."

"What's an advance?" I said.

"What do you need the advance for?" said Melissa.

"Are we in an interrogation room?" said Dad.

"I'm just asking," Melissa said. "What you need it for."

"For electricity," said Dad, tearing the plastic off some kitchen roll. "To make things nice and cosy. Christmas spirit and Christmas treats. And paper towels."

"What's an advance?" I asked again, but no one answered, and Dad went into the bathroom and turned on the taps.

That afternoon Melissa sat in bed, picking at her hands. After a bit, she got up and looked out of the window. Dad was in the kitchen and in the bathroom and in the living room, all the time he was in different rooms, and the afternoon went by, but no one made spaghetti. Then evening came. Dad stuck his head round the door.

"Okay," he said. "Just wanted to let you know I'm off out for a bit."

"Okay," Melissa said. "I'll come with you."

She got up and stood in the middle of the room, underneath the light bulb.

"Why?" said Dad.

"I was thinking maybe I'd get something from the shop," Melissa said. "You've had that advance, after all."

"What's an advance?" I said.

Neither of them looked at me. They were only staring at each other.

"It's money," Dad said.

"Money you get before the job is done," Melissa said. "Payment is what you get afterwards."

"Nothing wrong with enjoying yourself a bit, is there," Dad said. "Since it's nearly Christmas and all. Nothing wrong with having a bit of fun."

"Mm," Melissa said. "You were thinking of Stargate, were you?"

"Hm?" said Dad.

"You were thinking of having a bit of fun at Stargate?" Melissa said.

"No," said Dad. "I was thinking I might buy the two of you some Christmas presents, actually. Is that all right? Do I have your permission, Melissa?"

Melissa didn't say anything else after that, and Dad just stared at her until she had to look away, until she went and sat back down on the bed.

Afterwards, as I lay under the covers, I thought of all the things I should have done. I should have said, *but we don't want any presents this year.* I should have gone to Eriksen and said, *don't give our Dad an advance*, I should have knocked at Aronsen's and said, *can you look after Dad's wallet?* But I hadn't done any of that. I'd gone with Dad out into the hall, and stood there like a little idiot, going, *are you buying presents? Shall I tell you what I want, then?* And all at once I couldn't remember anything I really wanted, but I said things anyway, I said things I'd wanted ages ago, *a skipping rope*, I said, *a baby doll* and *felt-tip pens*, and Dad said, *yeah, sounds great.* But then he took his leather jacket off the hatstand and said, *all righty, girls, I might be a while. Got a few tabs to settle up as well.*

"Can I get into your bed?" I said.

Melissa nodded.

I curled up in her arms. A dog was barking outside the window.

"Life goes on," Melissa said.

"I should have said simpler presents," I said. "It won't be easy to get hold of all that stuff."

Melissa looked at me. Her eyes are so pretty, they're so murky.

"Especially at night," I said.

"He isn't buying presents," she said. "He's at Stargate. Or the Friend at Hand."

I curled up at that, hard, like a pebble.

"They should call that place the Enemy at Hand," I said.

Melissa turned onto her side. She pushed the hair back from my face.

"They should close that place down," I said.

"I used to think like that too," she said.

"What?" I said.

"I don't think like that anymore," she said. "It wouldn't help, you know. Remember when they barred him from Stargate? He just started going to the Friend at Hand. And if you're chucked out of the Friend at Hand, you just end up going to the supermarket."

She stroked my eyebrows with her index finger. First one, then the other. Outside, the dog barked over and over.

"That's the lady-man's mutt," Melissa said. "It never figures out how tiny it is."

I put my nose up against her neck. The dog barked and barked.

"So it's not something worth hoping for," Melissa said.

But I can't not hope. That's just the way my brain is. So I hope that someone smashes up Stargate, and shuts off all the beer taps in the world, but that will never happen, there's always beer flowing somewhere, so my mind went black. I had nothing to say. It just goes on and on. I just think and think and think, and then comes night, because it always does. It was the last night in November. I was lying still in the crook of my sister's shoulder.

Then there are days like these. I've had them before and I know they come, so I also know they end. I know exactly how: they end with Dad at the kitchen table, saying, *sorry, girls, things will be different from now on*, and Melissa opens a drawer and takes out a spoon, and Dad says, *girls, will you forgive me*, and I nod, and Dad says, *Melissa, you too?* and Melissa goes to the fridge and answers, *I don't really have much choice, do I?*

And we know it's over then. Then his hands shake, and when he holds the mug there are ripples in the coffee, but he looks up and says, *how about I fry some eggs and bacon?* Then he goes out to the shops and comes straight back again. The days grow light and the nights black and still. Then there are sandwiches. Then there are neat piles of bills and cheese and eggs and bacon. *Melissa Moonlight*, Dad says, *this is the last time, but do you think you could come over here a minute? Do you think you could make a call or two for me?*

And Melissa sits at the kitchen table and rings around and says several different things. Sometimes she says, *I'm afraid we simply didn't get the original bill*, and sometimes she says, *I'm afraid he's simply been knocked off his feet with this pneumonia*, and once she just said, *hello, two motherless children and an alcoholic here, can you please give us two more weeks?* And then comes spring or summer or autumn, and Dad gets a job and stands at the kitchen sink, washing up our lunch boxes, and at bedtime he comes into the room to say good night, and he pauses in the doorway and looks at us, patting down his pockets. *Where are my sunglasses*, he says, *you're hurting my eyes*. And after a while Melissa cheers up too. She starts going out at night. I can hear her laughing outside the window. I don't like that. But Dad says, *she's young, Ronja, why don't we play a game of cards?* And then there are summer evenings when it rains against the glass and we play casino at the kitchen table, or summer days when we pack our bags and go out to an island, and Dad and I smile at each other underwater, and Dad and I float out into the big sea and he looks up at the sky and says, *this is the way for kids to live.* Afterwards we sit at the water's edge, and he holds up a crab and takes one claw and shakes it, saying, *afternoon, afternoon,* so I don't get scared. Or it's autumn and dark and he's telling me about the cabin that we're going to have. He carries me into my room and says he's carrying me home through the snow, that we're in a big forest, but we're safe in our cabin. He puts me to bed and says the snow is piled several feet above the walls. He tucks the duvet round my legs. *There we go*, he says. *Lift up your little tootsies.*

That's how it ends.

But before it ends, it must go on. And it goes on with him losing this job or that job or another, and the fridge gets empty, and then the people come and sit on the sofa and say, *well, hello there, is that Ronja out and about?* and they say, *give us a smile*, and I don't answer, because what answer can you give to that.

"Do you believe it that he's coming home soon?" I said.

"Believing's for the mosque," Melissa said.

"But what do you think?" I said.

I was lying with my nose pressed up against her neck. Where I breathed it left a damp spot.

"I think you should go to sleep," she said. "Close your eyes. I can tell you all about that cabin."

There's got to be woodland with snow on the trees. And sometimes there's a little lake and sometimes there's a marsh, but always the path runs beneath stooped trees and always the woodland is unending, and always there's a cabin all alone, right at the heart. Go up to the doorstep, brush the snow off your clothes. Close the door behind you. That's it, then fasten the door with a hook, since no one's going out again that night, and outside hop hares and pad foxes, and in the distance howl wolves, but indoors, where we are, the fire burns while we sleep, and keeps until we wake. Then we just have to blow on the embers.

"Wake up," Melissa said.

I opened my eyes. It was light.

"I'm going now," Melissa said.

"Why?" I said. "It's Sunday."

She stood at the window, buttoning a shirt, a white one I'd never seen before.

"Yeah," she said. "But I'm going out."

I got up. The floor was cold. I went over to the window and saw what she saw. There was sun and frost on everything downstairs, and the lady-man was trotting around with the dog in a bag. Everything was in full swing, and I don't like waking up with everything already in full swing. There was Musse too, running helter-skelter down the street in his denim jacket, his dad behind him, probably on their way to mosque. They've got to go to mosque nearly all the time, and time is always getting away from them. I turned to Melissa. Her shirt was much too white. I don't like it when she goes places. And I don't like seeing Musse and his dad, because I envy those with faith in gods—they always know where they're going, they just run across the road beneath the mighty hand of God, but we don't believe in any gods. *Jesus was a great medicine man*, Dad likes to say, *that's all*, so I hardly ever know where I'm going, only one place comes to mind, and that's behind Melissa.

Melissa went out into the hall. I followed.

"Why are you going out?" I said. "Where to? What happened yesterday?"

She went into the bathroom. I sat down on the toilet lid.

"Sonja brought him home, that's all," she said.

She opened the cabinet and took out her makeup things. I pulled my T-shirt down over my knees. Leaning towards the mirror, she held her top and bottom eyelids apart and drew black makeup along the edge, her mouth open. And honestly, she didn't need to say much else. I could picture it. Sonja standing in the corridor outside in those stupid boots of hers, holding Dad upright, and she'd said *here we go, gently does it*, and then Melissa had had to say thank you as Dad tumbled into the flat.

"She explained what happened," Melissa said.

"But what did happen?" I said.

"What happened is he made an arse of himself," Melissa said. "You don't need to know the details."

She went into the hall. She laced up her basketball shoes, put on her coat.

"Come here," she said. "Is the back of my coat covered in a load of hair and stuff? Hairy clothes aren't considered appropriate when you're applying for a job."

"You're applying for a job?" I said.

"We're keeping this one in the family," Melissa said.

Then she wound her scarf around her neck. It was red. Afterwards she grinned at me in the mirror and said, "I'll get the job. They'll be desperate, they need people this time of year."

She leaned in towards the mirror, narrowing her eyes and leaning forward and back until she looked at me and said, "Do I look all right?"

"Yeah," I said. "Hair's a bit messy, that's all."

"Messy hair," my sister said. "I'm sure Herman Eriksen will like that."

And Herman Eriksen did. Or maybe he liked the makeup or the scarf, or maybe they were desperate, like Melissa had said. Whatever it was, she came back. It was night by then. She kicked off her shoes and dropped her coat on the floor. Then she went into the kitchen and said, "I got the job back."

She sat down at the table, rubbing her face.

"I started straightaway," she said. "Could you please get me some Frosties and a pair of dry socks?"

I got her Frosties and a bowl and spoon. I stood beside her like a waiter, pouring milk. She glanced up and said thank you, makeup all across her cheeks. I got sugar and socks. She scooped Frosties into her mouth with one hand and rested her forehead on the other.

Then she looked up.

"What?" she said. "What is it?"

"Aren't you happy?" I said.

"Oh," she said. "Sure."

She put the spoon down on the table. "I get paid less than Dad did. Plus I don't like begging."

"Nah, you didn't beg," I said.

"Oh yeah I did," Melissa said, lifting the bowl and drinking the rest of the milk.

"Oh yeah," she said again. "I begged."

Later, I lay next to her in bed. Her body was stiff.

"Those people drive me nuts," she said.

I poked my toes into her leg.

"They say they're doing us a favour," she said.

She twisted, kicking off the duvet. "And they're deducting Dad's advance from my pay," she said. "It's so fucking bright in here."

She got up in bed and started tugging at the roller blinds. She said she couldn't sleep with the headlights shining on the ceiling, but that blind hadn't worked in ages—she wrenched and tugged at it anyway, until at last something loosened at the top and the whole thing hung askew.

"There," she said, lying back down. "Brilliant."

She curled the pillow under her neck and closed her eyes. But she wasn't sleeping, I could tell.

"My head's full of trees when I close my eyes," she said. "Jesus fuck—they've brainwashed me."

"Yeah," I said.

"And I don't like what they said about it being a favour," she said.

"No," I said.

The dog barked outside. Melissa groaned.

"But aren't they doing us a favour, sort of?" I said.

At that she only groaned again.

After a while, I realised what they meant by a favour. It was her starting at six and working two hours before school, and after school she had to go back and work till closing. The boss said they were being flexible, but it wasn't true, Melissa said, *everybody knows the worst part is setting up the display in the dark when the trees are wet and cold, not swanning in at ten when the sun's up and everything's already sorted.* But whatever, that was how it had to be. Mornings and afternoons and holidays Melissa had to be there, that was the favour, and Dad's advance was deducted from her pay, and when the others came at ten the display had to be ready.

"There's no point anyway," she said. "Who buys a Christmas tree at ten in the morning? Who's going out and buying a Christmas tree after breakfast and hauling it along to the office?"

"Nobody," I said.

"But whatever," she said. "Tomorrow morning you'll have to sort yourself out. I've got to leave at six to set up the display."

"Okay," I said.

And after a while I said, "But what's the display?"

"Trees," Melissa said. "Everything at that job is trees."

"That sister of yours," the caretaker liked to say. "I won't forget her in a hurry. She ruled this playground practically single-handed."

"Melissa the Militia, yes," the caretaker liked to say. "I could have done with her fighting my corner back home."

When I woke up, she was gone. I went to school. They had us making Christmas decorations, and I got to be in a group with Musse and Meron, and we chose paper chains, but I couldn't even manage that, and Musse looked at me and said, *hey, what's up with you, you're gluing those together inside out.* Then school was over. I went home. But in the hallway I just stood there, still.

The flat was grey and empty. And I turned grey and empty too—there was nothing nice in there, the only nice thing was the hatstand we inherited from grandma, with brown curlicues, but otherwise there was nothing, and suddenly I couldn't stand to be in such a place. So I went back out again.

I went to the petrol station. Something had been sloshed across the ground out there, and the tarmac was full of puddles and rainbows. I looked towards the Christmas tree market. Over by a shed, two men stood talking. Melissa was running around among the trees, acting like she didn't see me, and her snowsuit was way too big, the legs hanging like two sausages. I sat down on a red newspaper box. Melissa was lifting trees off a pallet, measuring trees with a stick and pushing trees through a tunnel so they came out wrapped in netting. She didn't wave at me, not even once. In the end, though, she came over. By that time it was late afternoon.

"Go home," Melissa said. "It's stressing me out, you sitting there."

I shook my head.

"Go on," Melissa said. "People don't bring their brothers and sisters to work."

I said nothing.

"That Eriksen guy is nuts," Melissa said. "I can't even go for a pee when he's around."

But she couldn't make me leave. I just shook my head, and Melissa had to keep working. She wound her scarf around her neck and went.

Dusk fell, but I could see her still, because a floodlight hung above the market on a pole. After a long while it was night. Eriksen left. And finally Melissa finished too. She went into a shed and when she came back out she had her coat on, and she folded up a sign and leant it against a wall. She pulled out a plug and the market went dark. Then she came over to me.

She took my hand and we walked home together. She walked slowly. She was white in the face. She said nothing.

But afterwards, once I'd fetched dry socks and she'd got some Frosties and some milk and sugar in her, she stood in the bathroom and said it was a shitty job.

"People think Christmas trees are this happy-clappy thing," she said. "But the Christmas industry is full of shitty people. And my mittens are complete shit too, the needles go right through them."

I sat on the toilet lid. She shook the needles out of her hair into the sink.

"People don't realise how much fir trees stab you," she said. "And they have no idea how cold it is standing still and saying stuff like, *this one, madam, is that the one you prefer? Would it suit your living room?*"

She stuck her head under the tap and rubbed her face.

"Do you really say *madam*?" I said.

"What?" she said. "I can't hear anything down here."

"Do you really say *madam*?" I said.

She turned off the tap and looked up. She was dark around the eyes and the water ran down her cheeks. Her forearms were covered in small red dots. She looked like something from Halloween.

"That's not the point," she said. "The point is that I'm a slave."

Then she said that she was Tommy's slave, and Tommy was Eriksen's slave, and Eriksen, he was a slave too, he was just too stupid to realise, but he was a slave to Christmas and Jesus and Christianity, and for that matter the whole of Christianity was a slave to capitalism.

"Which is the problem," Melissa said.

"With what?" I said.

"With everything," Melissa said. "With absolutely everything."

The next day I went down there again. It had turned colder. The sky was pale blue and the exhaust fumes looked like cotton wool. I sat on the newspaper box, leaning the back of my head against the petrol station wall. I drew up my legs and rested my forehead on my knees. I lay down on my belly and kicked my feet in the air. Then someone touched my shoe. I twisted round. A man was standing there.

"Hello," he said. "You're the kid sister?"

He wore a snowsuit and huge black gloves. I sat up.

"Tommy," he said, holding out one glove. "Come on. Let's head on over."

"I can't," I said.

"It's fine," he said. "Eriksen's already left."

"Melissa doesn't want me to," I said.

"That's not up to her," said Tommy, putting his glove around my hand. "Come on. We're about to have a staff meeting."

And then he drew me with him in among the firs.

"Melissa," Tommy yelled. "Come here."

Melissa was sitting on the ground, midway through righting a fir. She looked up from underneath the branches and crawled out. She looked scared.

"Relax," Tommy said, "It was me who went and got her."

He walked over to the shed and opened the door.

"Take a seat," he said. "Have a ginger biscuit."

There was warmth inside, and a radio, and the floor brown with dirt. Some children singing "O Holy Night." I sat down on one camping stool, Tommy sat on the other. Melissa stayed standing in the doorway. *A thrill of hope*, sang the children. *The weary world rejoices.*

"Melissa," said Tommy. "Your sister can't spend all day sitting out there on a box when it's below freezing out."

"I know," said Melissa. "That's what I told her."

Tommy looked at me.

"Right," he said. "So what's up with you, then?"

Melissa was picking the needles out of her mittens. Tommy opened a tin of chewing tobacco and started shaping a pellet.

"Eh?" he said. "What's your deal?"

"I want to be here," I said.

"Right," said Tommy. "But here's the thing I'm wondering. Do you want a job, ladybird?"

Melissa glanced up at that. Under the woolly hat and with that messy hair, she looked like an animal.

"A job?" I said.

"Yeah. How'd you like to come and work for us?" Tommy said.

I glanced at Melissa, but she was looking only at Tommy.

"Work?" I said.

"All right then, listen," Tommy said. "Have you ever heard about commissions?"

Commissions were simple, Tommy said. He got paid a commission on decorative greenery, and decorative greenery, well, that was basically what regular people called wreaths. *It's just like with the trees,* Tommy said, *regular people call them Christmas trees, Eriksen calls them bushes.* So, he got paid a commission on decorative greenery and traditional sheaves of Christmas grain, and Tommy needed that commission, *since the missus is pregnant, so I could use a bit extra right about now.*

Melissa narrowed her eyes and leaned against the doorframe.

"Do you know how much a baby changing table costs?" said Tommy. "And I'm sure you don't need me to explain why we're not buying one secondhand?"

"And the point is?" said Melissa.

"The point is," said Tommy, "that if you two help me out here and there, I'll split the commission with you."

He smiled.

"But why?" Melissa said. "Why would you split it with us when you could keep the whole thing?"

"Because I've got a plan," said Tommy.

"What sort of plan?" said Melissa.

"Her," said Tommy, pointing at me. "She's my plan."

"Listen," Tommy said. "People buy trees, right. But what are they actually buying?"

"Bushes?" I said.

"You've got to think bigger," Tommy said. "What is it our customers need?"

"Bushes *and* decorative greenery?" I said.

"Bigger," Tommy said.

I nodded. Then I shook my head.

"Girls," said Tommy. "We're selling a dream. What our customers are buying here is the spirit of Christmas. And do you know what gives people more Christmas spirit than anything else?"

"Is this a quiz, or what?" Melissa said.

But Tommy wasn't looking at her, he was looking at me. His eyes were pale blue.

"Feeling like they've done a good deed," Tommy said.

He told us beggars were rushed off their feet at Christmas. He told us that the modern consumer no longer bought Christmas presents, they bought goats in Africa. He told us Africa was now chock full of goats and there was a queue outside the Salvation Army all December long, but it wasn't those in need of salvation who were queuing, said Tommy, it was rich folk desperate to find someone to help. *I mean*, Tommy said, *nobody wants to celebrate with their own family anymore, everybody wants to celebrate with the poor people and the junkies.*

I sucked on the ginger biscuit, turning it soft and wet and good.

"And you know what story people love to read at Christmas, don't you?" Tommy said. "'The Little Match Girl.' And you remember what it's about, don't you?"

I took the ginger biscuit out of my mouth.

"A Christmas tree," I said.

"A hungry little kid staring at a roast goose through a window," Tommy said, smacking the tobacco tin down on the table and nodding at Melissa. "Jesus fuck, as you say. *That's* what people call Christmas spirit."

"Yeah," I said.

"So then do you know who people most want to help at Christmas?" Tommy asked. "More than anybody else in the world?"

"No," I said.

"Skinny little kids," said Tommy.

"Skinny?" said Melissa.

"Yes," said Tommy, patting me on the head. "And that's where she comes in."

"Sheaves and wreaths!" I shouted. "Wreaths and sheaves! All proceeds go to children in need!"

It was the next day. All I had to do was stand there, that was my job, I had to stand on the pavement with a sheaf of grain in my arms and bring in customers to buy the decorative greenery, yes, all I had to do was look skinny and sweet and poor for Tommy to give us half the commission, and Melissa said there was no way anybody could be that stupid, but she was wrong.

People stopped in front of me all the time. They stopped and smiled and tilted their heads and took out their wallets, old housewives, young ladies, Stella's dad. They had mittens and bags and clouds of frost coming from their mouths, *well, goodness me*, they said, *will you look at that, some good old-fashioned Christmas sheaves, and such a lovely little girl*, and I smiled and nodded and said, *the till is over there*. Then it got dark, and Musse came running over too, wearing that nice denim jacket with a sheepskin collar. He stopped in front of me.

"You're here?" Musse said.

"Yes," I said. "I've got a job."

"You're always so lucky, you are," Musse said. "Is the money going to children in need?"

"Yes," I said. "Well, sort of."

"You're always so kind, you are," Musse said, and then he smiled and said, "See you at school."

And I smiled back, and Musse ran on, and I knew what he was going to tell the class, *Macaronja's got a job, man*, and I kept on selling, but in the end my legs got tired, and Melissa called and told me to come into the shed.

"You're a genius," Melissa said.

She'd taken my notebook out of my bag and sat there doing sums.

"Two hundred," she said. "Four hundred, six hundred, Macaronja, this is crazy. And pretty soon we'll be running out of decorative greenery."

Tommy came in. He shut the door behind him.

"Girls," he said.

"Tommy," Melissa said. "Ronja's a little genius."

"Girls," said Tommy, slinging his money belt onto the table. "This is great and all, it's great, but this kids in need stuff? Not sure that's on, really."

"But that was the whole idea," Melissa said.

"I know," Tommy said. "And it's fine to stretch the truth a bit. But she's broadcasting it practically across the whole of Tøyen."

We said nothing.

"The money isn't going to children in need," said Tommy. "It's going to Eriksen Firs. And Herman Eriksen and his wife go driving around in a convertible, swanning off to the countryside in the middle of winter—it's so stupid you wouldn't believe it."

"And the point is?" said Melissa.

"Yeah, well, the point," said Tommy, "is that they aren't in need."

"But us?" I said.

"Us what?" he said.

I didn't answer that. I wanted to let him think about it for a bit. He gazed at me with his pale blue eyes.

"You're going to be a dad too," I said.

"Do you think your kid's going to be rich?" Melissa said.

"And you don't want to buy a secondhand changing table, do you?" I said.

Tommy looked at me, and at Melissa, and back at me. "You might have a point there," he said.

I took another ginger biscuit. Melissa was slowly drawing a plus sign in the notebook.

And at last, Tommy nodded. "Let's run with it," he said. "But is there any way you could try and shout a little quieter?"

That day we earned two hundred each. Next day we earned three hundred each, and Melissa pointed at the numbers in the book and said, *look, that's your Christmas tree right there.* By the third day Tommy had bought a new changing table at Babyshop and the missus said he was an angel. And every day I ran to the petrol station after school. I stood behind the diesel pump, and if the sheaf was hanging off the corner, Eriksen was gone, and I ran up and got to work. And working, it's the very best thing a person can do.

When you're working. Then there's no need to think things and feel things and wonder things. And it was as though I couldn't hear the people in the living room when I heard them. It was as though I didn't see Dad when I saw him. So when they said, *give us a smile, eh, Ronja*, I just smiled, and when Dad said, *I didn't name you Ronja for you to grow up in Tøyen, kids shouldn't be living in a place where you can't see the starry sky*, I said, *it's all right, Dad*. I just went into the hall and took my jacket off the hatstand, because I had a job. And I liked smiling at the customers. I liked their wallets, I liked saying, *but how are you doing for decorative greenery?* And at the school gate the caretaker patted me on the head and said, *what you smiling about, you never used to smile like that*, but I couldn't help smiling, because I was thinking about wreaths and sheaves, and then I was shouting about wreaths and sheaves, and when I got tired, Melissa noticed straightaway, and she'd wave me down and tell me to sit on the steps, and Tommy fetched hot chocolate from the petrol station, *because you're a proper little cash machine*, he said, *and we've got to keep our cash machine well oiled.*

And in the evening, when we'd closed up and were sitting in the shed counting the take, Tommy told us about other Christmas tree sellers in other places. They were much nastier than us. They scammed old ladies who couldn't see the numbers on the measuring stick, they sold trees that looked like bottle brushes. And in Nittedal, said Tommy, it was all-out war. Two sellers there had been fighting since the nineties.

"And do you know what happened?" Tommy said.

I shook my head. Melissa was stacking coins into tall towers.

"One night, one of the sellers went out with a fire extinguisher," said Tommy.

"Why?" I said.

"Why do you think?" said Tommy. "By the time the other one showed up to work, his whole place was nothing but foam. Hundreds of trees, massive wastage. But do you know what the second one did the very next night?"

"What?" I said.

"The very next night he went out there with a chainsaw," Tommy said.

He picked up the thermos. Melissa looked up from the money.

"Anybody want the rest of the glögg?" Tommy said.

"But what did he do?" Melissa said.

"What do you think?" said Tommy.

"Did he saw up the trees?" I said.

Tommy nodded slowly. He poured the last dregs of glögg into my cup.

"And do you know who was working in Nittedal in the nineties?" he said.

"No?" I said.

"Well," said Tommy. "It was a fellow by the name of Herman Eriksen."

Then one day the sun was shining. I was sitting on the steps. Melissa stood by a pallet of mountain firs, pulling the netting off them and it was easy, because the trees were dry and soft. Tommy had gone to buy hot chocolate. At the top of a silver fir sat a blue tit, chirping. I shut my eyes. The sound reminded me of spring. The sun was shining on my eyelids, turning everything red. I leant my head against the door, my thoughts turning into dreams, and the bird chirped like a bird in a dream.

"Oy," said a voice.

I opened my eyes.

And there, right in front of me, was Eriksen.

Melissa straightened her back. Eriksen was turned away from me, his back short and broad. He looked at Melissa and jabbed his thumb at me, pointing over his shoulder.

"Why's she sitting there?" he said.

"Who?" said Melissa.

"Her," said Eriksen.

I wanted to stand up. I wanted to run. I wanted to disappear, that's what I wanted. Dear God, I thought, I don't want to be Ronja, I want to die, I don't want to be on a planet spinning through the universe, dear God, please just let the whole thing vanish all at once.

"It's a step, isn't it?" Melissa said. "Have you got something against people sitting on steps?"

Tommy came out of the petrol station. He hadn't seen us. In one hand he held a cup of hot chocolate, and a bag of rolls dangled from the other. Then he spotted Eriksen, and stopped swinging the bag. He walked more quickly, and came and stood beside Melissa. He was biting his lip.

"Tommy," said Eriksen. "People are saying there's a kid that works here."

"Huh," said Tommy. "People say some funny stuff."

The bird hopped down onto the ground and cocked its head.

"That many people don't say that much funny stuff," said Eriksen. "And people are saying there's a kid works at Eriksen Firs. They come to me and say, *I bought a wreath from that cute kid*, and at first I say, *that can't be right, it must have been somewhere else*, but then they say, *by the petrol station, isn't that where you sell your trees?*

"I see," said Tommy, nodding towards Melissa. "Well, that's what happens when you employ sixteen-year-olds."

"Yeah, sorry," said Melissa, smiling. "People tend to think I'm twelve."

Eriksen looked at her.

"Thirteen," she said.

"You listen to me," said Eriksen. "You two are the ones running the place. But I don't want to see her round here again. We're not in the business of child labour at Eriksen Firs."

"Got it," Tommy said.

Eriksen turned towards me. I stood up.

"You heard what I said," said Eriksen. "I don't want to see you here anymore."

"Got it," I said.

"This isn't a shelter or a refugee centre, all right?" he said.

"No," I said.

"So you're off home, then?" said Eriksen.

"Yes," I said. "Then I'm off home."

I went off home. I no longer had a job. I took the fire escape up. I opened the door upstairs, but then I saw Aronsen standing in the corridor outside our door, and our door was open so I heard what he was saying.

"It seems to me that this situation is starting to come off the rails," said Aronsen.

I stood still. It was as though I'd gone completely flat. It was as though I were a paper doll, but no one was holding me up anymore. I heard Dad's voice.

"What do you know about rails?" said Dad. "Aren't you a retired accountant?"

There was a crash in our hallway, maybe the hatstand falling over.

"Oh dear," said Aronsen.

After a minute, he shook his head. "Well, at any rate, you know my opinion," he said.

Then he shut our door and turned around and spotted me.

"Hello," said Aronsen.

"Hello," I said.

"You're heading home, I see," said Aronsen.

I nodded.

"Want to come over to my flat for a bit?" he said.

"I don't go round to strangers' flats," I said.

"No," said Aronsen.

I wasn't going anywhere as long as he was stood in the middle of the corridor. With that white hair of his on top.

"Where's your sister?" Aronsen said.

"At work," I said.

"And you have to go home, do you?" he said, and I couldn't bear him looking at me like that, I couldn't bear him saying things like that, or thinking them.

"No," I said. "I was just going to drop this off."

Then I went along the corridor. I dropped my bag on the mat. I didn't look at Aronsen, just marched on past and over to the other fire escape and opened the door and disappeared.

But I didn't disappear. It doesn't work like that. I just stood there staring at the red fire door, and didn't know where to go.

Then those days came. And I don't like those people on the sofa, I don't like Sonja saying, *goodness, is that Ronja out and about*, and saying how she also had a daughter once, and I don't like hearing how that daughter is a health worker now and never has time for Sonja. And I don't like the sound of Dad throwing up, because next day it makes my head feel weird, and I went to school and tried to keep up, but there was nothing there to keep up with, just shortbread and Santa Lucia songs, and Musse said *it's getting Christmussey in here*, but I didn't laugh. Then we were given a note about when the Santa Lucia celebrations were starting, and we spent the whole time singing "Hark! The Herald," and they spent the whole time talking about Santa Lucia costumes. It wasn't very fun. And at break time Musse said, *I don't see you at the Christmas tree market anymore*, and that wasn't very fun, and at lunchtime I stood out by the gate, it was cold, but there wasn't any snow, and the caretaker asked if I wanted some börek, but I wasn't hungry. I crumbled up the börek for the squirrel, but the squirrel looked sad, and no wonder, because it isn't very fun being the only squirrel in Tøyen. And one of those days as I was stood outside, Dad came walking by.

Tarmac and sun, plain old tarmac and sun. It was only just twelve o'clock. But Dad wasn't walking right, and I went burning hot, and I went freezing cold, and then he spotted me. He smiled and raised his hand, so I had to raise mine too. But I knew everyone could see out through the school gate. And I thought, just chop my head off. Come, floods and fires and storms, why can't the waters rise and fill the streets, or why can't everything just burn, because then he won't have time to think about Stargate and no one will have time to think of us, because we'll all be running through Tøyen from burning trees and things that fall, why can't everyone just be running like that, carrying their children on their backs?

But the sun was shining on the pavement. The children were shouting *red rover red rover*. The caretaker blew smoke towards the sky. And Dad stopped in the middle of the road and smiled and waved. Then he kept walking but he was moving funny, it looked as though he'd peed himself. I held my breath. After all, what was I supposed to say, what was the caretaker supposed to say, what were the others supposed to say, and Dad just waved, he never stopped waving. Then something happened behind him. Dad turned around. At first I couldn't see. Then I saw.

It was the lady-man's dog. It bounded up at Dad's legs. And then it was the actual lady-man. Standing at the pedestrian crossing, saying something to Dad. Dad gestured towards me with his arm. The lady-man shook his head. He put his arm across Dad's back and turned him around.

That's the way they walked. The three of them. The lady-man guided Dad with one hand and held the dog's lead with the other. That's the way they walked, to the corner by the shopping centre, and then they were gone.

I looked into the playground. People were running around the climbing frame and laughing and screaming. I leant against the pillar. It was like I'd just had PE. My heart thudded in my ears. The caretaker stubbed his cigarette out on the pillar.

"You have nothing to be ashamed of," he said.

He put the butt back in the pack.

"Hm?" I said.

"Drink is a hard taskmaster," he said.

But I don't want people seeing things and saying things about things. I don't want that. I don't want them thinking things and remembering things and knowing things.

"That has nothing to do with you," the caretaker said. "Everybody understands that."

"I don't know what you're on about," I said. "You don't even speak proper Norwegian."

The caretaker looked straight ahead. Break time went on and on. Thoughts knotted in my head. The caretaker said nothing, only put his hands in his pockets. But everything was knotted in me like a massive knot. The schoolbell rang. I made to walk in through the gate, when the caretaker laid his hand on my head. I stopped.

"Macaronja," he said.

He knocked on the top of my head. Like you'd knock on a door.

"Don't you have a hat at home?" the caretaker said. "It's starting to get cold, you know."

That night I couldn't sleep. I heard Dad in the bathroom. Then he was in the doorway, saying, *I'm off out for a bit*. He went, he didn't turn the key, and I heard his footsteps on the fire escape. I got up and locked the door. I should have been blind, and deaf. I lay back down again. All you can do is shut your eyes. And I shut my eyes, but the thoughts were still there, I should have been stupid, been brain-dead. After a while I heard Melissa unlock the front door. I heard her drop her bag, I heard the water in the shower, and then she came in and threw her towel on the floor.

"Hi," I said.

"Oh, you're awake?" she said.

She sat down on the edge of my bed. Her hair dripped onto the duvet.

"What's up?" she said.

"I do a lot of stupid stuff," I said.

"Kids do stupid stuff all the time," Melissa said. "That's the point."

"And Santa Lucia," I said.

"Oh yeah," she said. "Is that tomorrow?"

Her eyes were shiny. They're so pretty. She looked out of the window, the roller blinds still hanging at a slant.

"Don't think about it," said Melissa. "I'll sort it. By the time you wake up, everything will be fine."

"But how?" I said.

"I know I've got that old costume somewhere," she said. "It's in the attic. Or the wardrobe. I'll find it in the morning."

"Thanks," I said.

"And you want me to come, right?" she said, picking up my hair.

I remembered when she walked in the Lucia procession. They came walking down the corridors and I stood with Dad outside the woodworking room. It was dark. She wasn't at the front, but still, she was the real Lucia, everyone knew that. She was the only one who sang like you're supposed to sing, all the other voices trailed after hers. As she walked past us, she winked at me. Then they vanished, down the stairs, and Meron's mother turned to Dad and said, *are you proud? You should be.* And Dad answered, *thanks, but she doesn't get that from me.*

"Hm?" Melissa said. "Do you want me to come?"

"Nah," I said.

"I can ask for time off," she said.

"No," I said. "Don't do that."

"I can tell them I'm sick," she said, and she picked up my hair again and let it go bit by bit between her fingers. "You have such lovely hair."

"Nah," I said. "Then you won't make any money."

"Okay," she said. "But at least you'll have a costume. Do you want to lie down with me for a bit?"

I lay in the crook of her shoulder and felt sleep come. And I remembered when we were at Camp Otter and Dad was doing a dry summer and only drinking tea outside the tent, and Melissa made a friend and we sat on a wall by the kiosk and unwrapped chewing gum. They let me hang out with them the whole time. The gum was in pink paper, and there were stickers of different dogs inside the packets.

The sun went down above the treetops. The friend had freckles all across her face, and she said loads of clever things, *what is a soul, really*, she said, and *people say the universe is infinite, but how can a thing be infinite?*

She got us thinking about all sorts. Way out in space and deep inside the brain, *do you know the problem with us human beings*, she said, *we're smart enough to ask, but just marginally too dumb to answer.* I got to keep all their stickers. They bought the gum for the taste, but I bought it for the dogs, I was thinking about the dogs that whole time. The gum smelled like strawberries, and the friend said, "If you had to choose between only being asleep and only being awake, which one would you pick?"

"Sleep," Melissa answered.

"You mean that?" said the friend.

"Of course," Melissa said. "Get out of all that hassle? Of course I mean it."

"Ladybird," Melissa said. "Wake up."

I opened my eyes. It was dark. She stood in front of me, holding something white.

"I told you I'd sort it," she said. "Here it is."

I sat up. It was cold. My heart was thudding hard.

"Is that a Lucia costume?" I said.

"It's just a bit creased," Melissa said. "Go round to Aronsen's and ask if he can iron it for you."

"Aronsen's?" I said.

"Yeah," she said. "If anybody round here's got an iron, it's him."

"But can you knock for me?" I said.

"Ronja," she said, "I've got PE first thing, and before that I've got to set up the display. I'm *this* close to failing PE. Please. You can handle knocking on a door."

I got dressed quickly, in the dark. I carried the costume and walked through the living room, where Dad was asleep on the sofa. The smell was bad. I went across the corridor and knocked at Aronsen's.

He answered, and somehow he's about ten miles tall, so I had to crane my neck. He held a cup of coffee in his hand.

"Sorry," I said. "Could you iron my Lucia costume, please?"

"Iron it?" he said. "Now?"

"Yeah," I said.

"It's six o'clock in the morning," he said.

"Yeah," I said. "But today is Lucia day."

I held the costume out towards him. I was freezing—it was cold in the corridor, and very bright and still. His hair was combed. It looked as though he'd been awake a long time.

"You can see it needs ironing," I said.

He took the costume out of my hands.

"It does look like it could do with a quick go on the board," he said. "Come on in, let's see what we can do."

I went into his front hall. I heard Melissa running down the fire escape. I glanced up. It was Aronsen, after all, who'd written that note, *kindly use the purpose-built stairwell*, but he looked normal and said nothing, only locked the door behind me.

"Right," he said. "Why don't you join me in the kitchen."

We went into the living room, where there was wall-to-wall carpet, and he walked through the kitchen door.

"Do have a seat," said Aronsen.

I sat down. I couldn't think of anything to say. Across the window hung a lace curtain, outside the streetlamps were lit, and way over by the shopping centre I saw Melissa running, her bag leaping on her back. Aronsen opened a tall cupboard and unfolded an ironing board. He filled the iron with water. The handles on his tap looked like flowers. Then he set about ironing. He ironed with the very tip. It looked as though he ironed every scrap of lace.

"If a thing's worth ironing, it's worth ironing well," said Aronsen.

I nodded. It was beginning to smell sweet. After a while he said, "You're supposed to be at school by half past eight?"

"Yeah," I said. "That's the dress rehearsal. Then there's the performance."

"When is that?" said Aronsen.

"Four," I said. "You're welcome to come."

"Thank you," said Aronsen.

He turned over the Lucia costume and held it up.

"Have you had breakfast?" said Aronsen.

"Yes," I said.

He was behind the costume, so I didn't see his face.

"But it was a little while ago," I said.

"Might be time for a snack, then?" Aronsen said. "You'll find what you need over there."

That was how the morning went. Weird. I sat at the table, which was grey and shiny, and ate slices of bread with cumin cheese and sausage. *Just help yourself*, he said. He had white bread, and I loved that, and he ironed very slowly, the sleeves and the nooks and the crannies, as the sky grew pink above the shopping centre, and I ate snack after snack, because when someone says *just help yourself*, I help myself. I looked at the clock above the door. The seconds ticked by.

"You don't need to keep an eye on the time," said Aronsen. "I'm a precise man."

I looked out of the window instead.

"So what's it all about, then, Lucia day?" said Aronsen.

Then all of a sudden I got chatty, must have been the sausage that did it, and I told him how the shortbread was free and Musse said things were getting Christmussey, I told him how the caretaker had bought a spotlight and when we got to "Hark! The Herald" he was going to light each of us up, one by one.

"And that's my favourite carol," I said.

"A classic," Aronsen said.

And as I was about to go, he gave me a hanger for the costume.

"There's no sense ironing something just to crumple it up in a bag," he said.

He stood in the corridor and held the costume while I went to fetch my bag. I locked our door, and Aronsen gave me the costume, and I went down the corridor with it like a banner or a shield. It glowed white. I held it high. And when I put it on, in the changing rooms before the dress rehearsal, it felt as though it was still a little warm.

But then came afternoon. And the world is just the world, of course, with pavements and climbing frames and parents who bring ginger biscuits in a tin. It doesn't help, swapping T-shirts for Lucia costumes. It doesn't help, the teacher coming round and putting glitter on our heads and saying, *there we go, lovely*. It's always hope that ruins everything, but I just couldn't get the stupid hope out of my head. Stella had a red ribbon around her midriff, and I stood behind the stage curtain, listening to the parents in the auditorium, the babies crying and chairs being moved around, and Stella leant towards me, *I can hear the twins*, she said, *that's the twins crying right now.*

The caretaker pulled the rope. The curtain went up. And there I was, staring. I stared from face to face, and none of them was Dad, so then I knew for sure, really, but I didn't stop, somehow I kept on hoping anyway. People can be late sometimes, after all. People can wake up suddenly and see the note on the fridge and run all the way to school, or they can bend down among rows of chairs to tie their shoelaces. So I kept staring, and hands waved and flashes flashed, but finally, finally, the caretaker turned all the lights towards the stage. After that I couldn't see anything anymore.

All is calm, we sang, *all is bright*. And I sang, I did, but my throat was hurting, *the stars are brightly shining*, I sang, *O hear the angel voices*, and then the music teacher came out and said, *and now we're going to hear what many people think is the most beautiful Christmas song of them all, "Hark! The Herald Angels Sing,"* and the caretaker stood by the curtain and put his hand to his heart and winked at me. Sometimes he just doesn't get it. That song isn't nice when you've lost your job, and I couldn't help but think of Dad, of how he says the world is broken, but honestly I don't agree, because honestly I think that song is true. I remembered when we got off at the wrong island and ended up somewhere full of pennywort, and I remembered Camp

Otter, where you could stand on the beach and watch the sun go down and all the lake turn pink, and I remembered the cabin in the woods. Every time I blinked, I remembered that. Melissa says I let my imagination run away with me, but it's not imagination if it exists—it happened, he'd been at Sunsted all summer and got better, he'd worked at the bakery all autumn and got rich, and then it was winter and we took the bus a long long way out of the city, and we walked a long long way into the woods, and deep inside there was the cabin he had rented, and he wore the woolly jumper, and he shovelled the snow away from the door, and we went in, and when he opened the door in the morning everything out there glittered, and he called out, *hello, blue tit! Hello, snowdrift! Hello, sky!* And I do think blue tits are nice, and cities and lawns too, and when Aronsen forgets to weed the triangle outside the block and the lawn goes yellow all over with dandelions, that's nice as well, but it's horrible to sing about, and then the spotlight came.

The beam hit us one by one. And people started whispering in the auditorium, the names of all their children. They were whispering so loud. And the light got to Meron and I heard his mother's voice, and the light got to Musse, and the light got to Stella, and then, then the light got to me.

But no one sees a note and just stops drinking. And it doesn't take that long to tie a shoe. So no one whispered *Ronja*, no one whispered *Robber's Daughter*, no one whispered and no one yelled and no flashes flashed, and the spotlight dazzled me, and two thousand years went by somehow, and I couldn't stop remembering—him smiling at me underwater that summer, and me lying on the rock, him drawing on my back with a piece of straw, and the cabin in the woods, the way he fastened the door with a hook and said that no one would be going out again that night, and finally, finally, the light moved off my face, but then the long bit started up with just the music. And the caretaker started shining a light on the audience. Then I had to look again. I didn't want to, but that's the way my eyes are, it's impossible to stop them. They went from face to face to face. I saw them all. A father holding up a camera. A mother crying and wiping her face. An old man, his back bolt straight, in a shirt and tie. And the old man closed his eyes as the light reached him, and the old man didn't cry, and didn't wave, and didn't smile, and the old man there was Aronsen.

All the light was back on us. The final verse began. And I grew lighter in my body, *peace on Earth*, I sang, at the top of my voice, because my throat wasn't hurting anymore, *joyful all ye nations rise*, I shouted, and Stella stared, but I didn't care, and the song finished, and the applause came, and I waved. Aronsen looked straight at me and nodded. I lifted up my other hand and waved with both. He nodded one more time.

"Who are you waving at?" said Stella.

"Aronsen," I said.

"Who's that?" said Stella.

"That's my granddad," I said.

"You call your granddad by his last name?" said Stella.

"Yes," I said. "That's the custom in our family."

I climbed down off the stage. The auditorium smelled of coffee. Everybody had somewhere to go, but I did too. My Lucia costume moved around me as I walked, and Aronsen was standing by the row of chairs, tall as a lighthouse. You could see him from anywhere.

"That went really well," he said.

"Thanks," I said.

"Joyful all ye nations rise," said Aronsen. "Very true."

The little kids were clattering around us, and chairs were scraping, and people were talking, but we just stood there. He said nothing else. I got embarrassed looking at his face, so I stared directly at his belly instead.

"I like the stars on your tie," I said.

"Oh, thank you," Aronsen said.

"Is that an Advent tie?" I said.

"Excuse me," Stella said.

I turned around. There she stood. She held a piece of shortbread in her hand. Her friends stood behind her, I didn't have to check, they always do.

"Excuse me," she said. "Is it true that you're Ronja's granddad?"

Aronsen looked down at me. He opened his mouth. I shut my eyes. I thought of all the school days still to come. I went to Stella's once, I know all the things she's got. A fancy wooden house. And two balconies and three cats, and her name means star and she says so all the time, and she's never not got someone home with her, her mum picks her up at two every day, and the twins are lying there with a stuffed bunny each and everybody wants to peer into the buggy—why couldn't she let me have a granddad when she has all that? But, whatever, anyway, why did I fib? I took a breath, I thought *please please please*, and peeped out between my eyelashes, but Aronsen wasn't looking at me anymore. He tugged at his tie, just below the knot.

"Why do you ask?" he said.

"Because Ronja said so," Stella said. "But if you are then it's a bit weird we haven't heard about you before."

"I see," said Aronsen. "And you'd like to know the truth?"

"Yes, please," said Stella.

She smiled.

"Well, perhaps there's a reason why she doesn't tell you everything," said Aronsen.

"Hm?" said Stella.

"It may be that my grandchild prefers talking to other people," said Aronsen.

Stella opened her mouth. And I realised I loved Aronsen. I loved his shirt and tie and his tall tallness, and all the notes he'd put up and all the times he'd knocked, I wished he was headmaster, or God, I wished he was the chairman of the housing board.

"Did you have any further questions?" Aronsen said. "Or are we finished here?"

Stella stood there. Mouth open, shortbread lowered.

"I think we're finished here," I said.

Aronsen nodded.

"Come, my grandchild," he said. "I need a cup of coffee."

We went. We went over to the cake table, because we were finished there, and the whole world smelled of coffee, and in the middle of the crowd, Aronsen stopped.

"Just a moment," he said.

He touched my hair. Then he patted the top of my head.

"That's better," he said. "You had your glitter all skew-whiff."

That was where the happy ever after started. Because the next day Eriksen left for Moss, to help his brother with the market there, and he wouldn't return till later in the week, so Tommy called Melissa and said I could come back, I could keep warm in the shed and do my homework and sell as much as I wanted, *because I know a thing or two about fathers myself,* he said. And the sheaf hung by the corner, and the floodlight shone, and there was frost on the needles of the firs, those were the good days, and I shouted about wreaths and sheaves and needy kids, and when I got cold I sat down with my homework folder at the camping table. I love camping tables. The homework was about emperors, there was Caligula and Nero and another one, and people hated them all, and I love it when people hate people, and on the radio they were talking about a storm that was supposed to come, its name was Gudrun and it was coming closer and closer from somewhere up north, and I love storms, and I love glögg and money, and in the afternoon we took a break, and Tommy went to buy doughnuts. Then we sat in the shed and ate them. They were still warm, and shiny with grease.

"Shall I tell you about when the missus got pregnant?" Tommy said.

"Um, maybe not?" Melissa said.

"Not like that," said Tommy. "Get this."

"You know that guy Alfred," Tommy said.

He tipped the camping chair backwards, resting the back of his head against the wall.

"Yeah," I said. "We know him."

"Really?" Tommy said.

"Well, sort of," I said.

Melissa was laying out hundreds in a fan across the table.

"Anyway, he's a funny bloke," Tommy said. "One time back in June we were clearing some forest in Enebakk, and we were sitting on a log taking a break, and then he just goes, *hey, congratulations, mate, you're going to be a dad*. But I wasn't going to be a dad, so I just said, *what are you talking about?* But he didn't answer, just slapped on his hearing protection and started up the saw. But you know what? When I got home, the missus was pregnant."

"Huh?" I said.

"She was pregnant," Tommy said, tipping the chair forward again. "She'd peed on that stick thing."

"Too much information," Melissa said.

"But how did Alfred know?" I said.

Tommy shrugged. "Don't know," he said. "But he was the one who told me. He's like that, you know. Psychic."

"Right, he's like the angel Gabriel," Melissa said. "He's like, *Tommy, son of David, unto thee shall be born a child?*"

But Tommy smiled and patted her on the head, and Melissa squirmed away and said his fingers were all greasy, but then he pinched her cheek and said, "You think you're so canny, don't you, Miss Melissa. But there are more things between heaven and earth than commissions and Christmas decorations."

And then I spotted Aronsen among the mountain firs.

I threw the doughnut onto the table and ran out and slipped on the ice and skidded in front of him, white smoke coming from my mouth.

"Aronsen!" I shouted. "Silver or ordinary?"

"Well, bless my soul," Aronsen said. "You're here too?"

"I've got to be here if I'm working here, haven't I?" I shouted. "Are you looking for a tree?"

"Well," said Aronsen, "I think I'm mainly after decorative greenery."

"Oh," I said. "And you know it's called decorative greenery?"

But then I remembered I was selling, and said, "I suppose you'll want some recommendations?"

I took his elbow and led him off towards the stand. And Aronsen nodded and thanked me and studied the wreaths while I fetched the sheet and showed him the prices, so he would know he wasn't being ripped off. *That one there's a moss rosette, you see*, I said, *that one there's a classic wreath, you see?* and Aronsen chose the ones I recommended, one for himself and one for his sister. Then he cleared his throat.

"Right," he said. "I need a headstone wreath as well."

"Has somebody died?" I said.

"Lots of people," Aronsen said. "But this one is for Mrs. Aronsen."

"Oh," I said.

"You can say that again," said Aronsen.

But he had an achy back, all old folk do. He looked quite tottery as he walked, holding a wreath in each hand and the one for the headstone under his arm. It was like he hadn't any balance in him.

"Stop," I shouted. "It's dangerous!"

Then I ran behind the shed and fetched a bucket of gravel.

"Which way do you want to go?" I said.

"Over there, I suppose," Aronsen said.

So I picked up the spade and shovelled gravel before his feet. And between each step I looked up and smiled. And between each step he smiled back at me. And so we walked, *let's take it very easy*, I said, and the gravel crunched as it hit the ground, *no rush*, I said, and I shovelled on, all the way up to the pavement, and there he nodded to me and said, *well, look at that for service.*

Yes, those were the good days. When I got back, Tommy was on the phone. He put it on speaker and I heard Eriksen, he said there was trouble at Moss, the silver firs hadn't come in, and now he had to drive the length and breadth of Østfold finding bushes. *I might just have to stay down here*, said Eriksen, and Tommy said, *oof, no, oof, no*, and gave me a high five, and once he'd hung up he asked if we could get started with something he'd been thinking about for a while.

"Home delivery," said Tommy, smiling.

"Christmas trees for home delivery!" I shouted. "Christmas trees for home delivery, Christmas discount!"

Melissa said I had to put a jacket on, but I didn't need it, I was baking hot in just my hoodie, and my breath was white and my heart beat hard, because Tommy was right, the modern consumer loved home delivery. The modern consumer was fussy and hoity-toity and didn't like to carry the tree home and didn't want needles in the car, and we aren't stupid, nobody can say that—I smiled with my head at an angle, and Melissa chatted to the modern consumer and said, *we do have an offer on home delivery today, as it happens, might that be of interest?* And Tommy loaded trees into his car and drove away, and we earned loads of money and bought loads of food, and at school the squirrel was over the moon because I had Maryland cookies in my lunch box, and he hopped around my feet all smiley.

Melissa was cheerful too. She wouldn't say so, but I saw it. In the evenings she stood at the kitchen counter grating cheese, going, *ow, my back, ow, my hand, Jesus fuck, I've got spruce needles in my knickers*, but then she'd sit down at the table and pour Nesquik into milk. *I like conning people*, she said, *I always have*, and after all that she stood under the shower for thirty minutes and said, *central heating. It's God's gift to humankind.*

"Standing out here, are we?" the caretaker said.

It was the last day of school. I was standing outside the school gate, thinking about money. I was thinking about the Christmas present I was going to buy Melissa, thermal mittens, really warm ones, and everything was leaping here and there inside me, but I stood where I always stood, answered as I always used to answer.

"Yes," I answered.

"You know that's not allowed?" the caretaker said.

"Rules are made to be broken," I answered, and then he lit his cigarette, and we went through the whole process of what was and wasn't allowed, but afterwards we didn't say anything.

It was very dark that day. And quiet on the streets, the quiet before Storm Gudrun, I suppose. The end of the cigarette glowed red in the strange dark. We ate the börek. The squirrel came and sat beside my foot.

"So, Ronja," the caretaker said. "Christmas coming up."

I nodded.

"What have you got planned?" he said.

"Bit of work," I said.

"Right. Seen anything of Alfred, have you?" he said.

I shook my head. The caretaker turned away and coughed for ages. When he turned back, he had strange eyes, shiny. I didn't know what to say.

"The squirrel's on good form today," I said.

Then the bell went. The caretaker put his hand on my head and knocked. The way you knock on a door.

"You take care, Ronja," he said.

"What?" I said. "What are you saying it like that for?"

"Ah, what for?" the caretaker said. "I'm just the Balkans' most melancholy man, I suppose."

It was the day before the day before Christmas Eve. Melissa had gone out by the time I woke. Dad was on the sofa, shaking his head. But it was like I had armour on. I just said, *take care, Dad*, and strolled right past him, breathing through my mouth while I did it, then I went out into the hall and put my shoes on, and in the corridor I breathed normally again, and that's when I smelled bacon. I didn't stop to think. I went right up and knocked on the door.

Aronsen opened it and looked down.

"Good morning," he said.

"Good morning," I said. "It smells of bacon in here."

"Does it?" he said.

"I was just scared you'd forgotten a pot on the boil," I said.

"A pot on the boil?" he said.

"Or a pan on the hob," I said. "I don't want you dying in a house fire."

"Ah, I see," said Aronsen.

"You know how old people forget things," I said. "They die in house fires all the time."

"Absolutely," said Aronsen.

We stood there. He wore a white shirt, very smooth around the buttons.

"Lovely ironing," I said.

"Oh, you're too kind," he said.

"But are you frying bacon, though?" I said.

"I am indeed," said Aronsen. "Shall I put on a rasher or two for you?"

Anyway, that's how it goes. You live happily ever after. Then you're happy and warm and full. Then you get slow. It's not like that in the fairy tales, but it is like that in real life, and we'd earned several thousand with the home delivery, and Tommy was talking about buying a dress the missus could wear once she stopped being pregnant, a red one, and then it was the day before the day before Christmas Eve and I was full and warm and rich, sitting on the steps outside the shed and watching everything. Evening came. The cars began to glisten. Melissa dragged the trees through the packing tunnel, Tommy nodded and smiled and said, *it's beginning to look a lot like Christmas*, and carried trees to the car and opened the boot, and every time he did, I took out my notebook and drew a line. After a while my toes got cold, so I went inside and ate a ginger biscuit. My homework folder was still on the table. I drew a handlebar moustache on Caligula, then I opened the notebook and looked at the accounts, home delivery on one page and decorative greenery on the other. I drew hearts around the numbers. Then the door opened.

"A-*ha*," said Eriksen.

He was in Moss. But no, he wasn't. He'd come back—he was stood right there in the doorway.

Maybe he had never even gone to Moss. Or maybe someone had called him and said, *I hear you've started doing home delivery at Eriksen Firs.* Or maybe he had spies in Oslo, and some lady had come up to Melissa and said, *I was just wondering about one of those mountain firs*, but out of the corner of her eye she'd seen the car and the open boot, or maybe someone had heard Melissa saying, *you'd like home delivery, absolutely, how's it looking today, Tommy?* And then Eriksen probably leapt into his car, he probably hightailed it up from Moss and parked that stupid convertible in a completely different place from normal and sneaked into the market like a fox, and now he was standing in the doorway, and he turned around and stuck his head out.

"Oy," he shouted. "Tommy! Melissa!"

I stared down at the table. I heard them coming. Eriksen shut the door behind them. It was much too cramped.

"All right," said Eriksen. "Explain."

"I'm just doing a bit of homework," I said, pointing at the homework folder.

"Homework?" said Eriksen. "It's two days before Christmas Eve."

"Extra homework," I said.

"Right. Yeah. Sure," Eriksen said.

He looked at Melissa. She clenched her jaw. Her fingers were moving. That's the trick she learned from Grandma. *Count to ten*, Grandma used to say, *it would do most people a world of good. But especially you.*

"Regardless," Eriksen said. "The kid can't sit here in the shed doing homework every day."

I saw Melissa do her second trick then, the one she learned from Dad. It's walking away from the person you're angry with. *There'll be idiots everywhere you go*, Dad used to say, *it's all about keeping your distance*, but as there wasn't anywhere for her to go, she backed into the clothes hanging on the wall.

"She doesn't," Tommy said. "This was a one-off."

Eriksen looked at him.

"She was feeling a bit under the weather today, that's all," said Tommy. "She needed a paracetamol and a bit of help with her homework."

"I wasn't talking to you," said Eriksen.

Then Melissa did the trick we had both learned from the caretaker. It's shutting your eyes. *Some things you just don't need to see*, the caretaker used to say, he found that out during the war, and Melissa screwed her eyes shut, but she was trembling, and that's the very last trick she knows.

"I'm tired of seeing that kid every time I turn around," said Eriksen.

At that Melissa opened her eyes. She lifted her chin and walked towards him.

"That kid is my sister," said Melissa.

"I didn't hire your sister," Eriksen said. "She's underage, big-time."

"We're a package deal," Melissa said. "Anywhere I go, she's welcome too."

"I think there's something you're forgetting," Eriksen said. He tucked his thumbs into his belt loops. "You're a pity hire," he said. "I gave you this job as a favour."

"Oh really? But now my little sister isn't feeling well and she comes here to ask for a paracetamol and maybe do some homework, maybe learn a bit about . . ." Melissa said, putting out her arm and picking up my homework folder.

". . . Emperor Nero," she said. "And now you're not doing us a favour anymore? Run out of pity, is it?"

Eriksen didn't reply.

"I'm asking if you have any paracetamol in your first aid kit?" Melissa said, tossing the homework folder back on the table. "But maybe you don't give paracetamol to underage kids?"

"Paracetamol?" said Eriksen. "This isn't about paracetamol."

"Maybe not for you," Melissa said. "But that's because you've never had a paediatric migraine. When you do, if there's one thing your entire life does become about, it's paracetamol."

Silence. Tommy fiddled with his money belt.

"Headache or no headache," Eriksen said, "this isn't a hospital."

"Of course," Tommy said. "It was a one-off."

"Okay," said Eriksen.

Tommy kept poking at his money belt, making the little zip tinkle. At last, Eriksen took a breath.

"But the next time I see her here, I'm calling someone," he said.

"Who?" I said.

Everybody looked at me.

I shouldn't have said it. It didn't sound like I had a paediatric migraine. Eriksen smiled.

"There are lots of people you can call," said Eriksen. "The important thing is that someone takes an interest."

But the worst thing is when someone takes an interest. I've always known that. That's when you're stuck crying into a sea of crabs. And I remembered the worst summer of my life, when Dad was at Sunsted and Melissa and I had to go to Superkids, and it was impossible to sleep with beams like that on the ceiling, and it was impossible to play red rover on the lawn, and I had to hold my tears back all the time, and I missed Dad until it felt like pneumonia in my chest. And when we fished for crabs, I sat on the outermost rock where no one could see. Nobody did see. They just shrieked and cheered about their crabs, but I didn't want to pick up even one, I let them eat the whole mussel while I cried and looked down at them. Until this guy called Kevin came balancing towards me on the rocks. He put his hand on my shoulder.

"Why don't you come inside and have some squash," he said. "I think that's enough crab fishing for today."

Eriksen hustled us out the door. We had nothing more to say. Outside there was darkness and a sort of noise in the air, must have been the sound of Storm Gudrun. Melissa and Tommy had to keep working, someone had dumped a pile of new silver firs by the curb. *We're two days out*, said Eriksen, *you keep going as long as there are customers.*

"And another thing," said Eriksen, holding out his hand. "From now on, I'll lock up the shed when I leave."

Tommy put the key into his palm.

I opened the door back home. The leather jacket was on the hatstand. I went into the living room. Dad was on the floor.

"Dad," I said.

He was lying by the wall. He lay on his back, with his face and his body, he lay just where the Christmas tree should have been. And suddenly I thought, I could kick him. I could stomp on his face. And I began to shudder.

"Why are you lying there?" I said.

He opened his eyes. Then he closed them again. I went further into the room.

"Dad," I said. "Why are you lying there in all that mess?"

But he wasn't awake anymore. And I shuddered again. Something black came into me, filling me up from below, and then it came out of my mouth.

"Why can't you ever buy vacuum cleaner bags?" I said.

I went a little closer.

"And how am I supposed to buy vacuum cleaner bags when I don't even know what the vacuum cleaner is called?" I said. "And when I don't even know where to buy them?"

Then I talked more loudly.

"And why can't you at least open a window when it stinks this bad?" I said. "You just make it stink everywhere," I said, and Dad just lay there, but the words leapt like frogs out of my mouth, and it felt so strange and lumpy, it had never happened before.

"And this ugly flat," I said. "With nothing but a hatstand to decorate it? And that leather jacket of yours, that smells like shit too," I said. "I bet you peed on it and everything. Why can't you even look where you're peeing?"

And I went all the way up and stood by his arm.

"Dad," I said. "You know I could drop something heavy straight on top of your head right now?"

I thought about the frying pan, but that made me think of bacon, the way he fried eggs and bacon saying, *girls, will you forgive me*, and that made me think of the kitchen table and how we played casino there, and how he always slipped me the two of spades, and when I thought about that I couldn't help but start crying, and I shook my head, because I saw it all right then, I saw it all, but there was nothing to be done, and I went into the hall and took the jacket off the hatstand and threw it on the floor, and took it up again and held it close to me and smelled that smell and gagged, because it wasn't all right, nothing was all right, and my tears ran down my neck and funny sounds came out of me, and I hung the jacket on the hatstand and went back to him and sat on the floor and leant my forehead against his arm and said, *sorry, Dad, will you forgive me*, but he was asleep, and I cried, his arm got wet, his arm smelled of Dad, and I cried and made funny sounds until I was exhausted. Then I went into my room to sleep.

But that night I wasn't well.

Thoughts began to run circles in my head. At first I thought they were just ordinary thoughts. Then I realised it was fever, so I lay very still. And my brain showed me pictures. There were blue tits and squirrels and crabs. There was cold and darkness and all the stars in the Big Dipper. I pulled the duvet over me and peered up at the ceiling and wondered what it was all supposed to mean.

"What's the matter with you?" Melissa said.

It's bright outside, it's morning. Her hair is hanging over me.

"You'd better stay home today," she says.

Her hands smell of spruce. She puts one on my forehead.

"No," I say.

"Yes," she says.

I'm too tired to answer that.

"You're probably just coming down with a cold," Melissa says. "Lie here and get better, all right?"

It's dark out, I'm alone.

But what's the matter with me? Is it paediatric migraines maybe, did we jinx it? See, here comes the headache. It comes like water, and the water rises in my head. I sit up and lean forward, but then everything gathers in my forehead, rolling like waves. And now I know what's happened. It's a punishment. This is my punishment. Because I thought that thing about the frying pan, and you shalt honour your father and your mother, and you shalt not kill, and you shalt not lie, nor shalt you steal, not you, and not you, and not even you, Brutus my son.

Paracetamol, paracetamol, paracetamol. And Eriksen's orange first aid kit, which opens again and again, and everything inside it is lined up nice and neat. I reach my hand out but it closes, it closes up again and again and slips out of my hands, and I open my eyes. My duvet, my hands. I'm just here. Here is where I am. But now there are people in the living room, there's music. And I get up, and the bedroom wobbles up and down around me like a sea. I've got to stand still, holding tightly to the bed. The wobbling stops, and I take a few steps and push open the door.

"Well, hello there," says Sonja. "Is that Ronja out and about?"

"Dad," I say. "My head hurts."

"Ooh, you poor thing," says Sonja.

And somebody says, *do you want to lie here on the sofa*, somebody says, *your daughter is talking to you*, somebody says, *turn the music down*, but nobody turns the music down.

"Dad," I say. "Do you have a paracetamol?"

Dad smiles. He gets up off the sofa and winks. He sways. Then he sits back down again. And Sonja shakes her head and says, "Wait a minute, sweetie."

She rummages in her bag, takes out a box.

"Here," she says. "This is a painkiller."

"Dad," I say. "Do you have any squash?"

Sonja gets up and takes my hand. "Come on, sweetie," she says, and heads towards the kitchen.

But I'm not her sweetie, but I have to have a paracetamol, and at the kitchen counter she lets go of my hand, she stands at our sink and makes squash. Somebody turns off the music. There is silence.

"Can't go wrong with cold squash, you know," says Sonja. "Can't go wrong with a nice bit of cold squash."

I nod. My brain is butting against the walls of my head. And Sonja opens the box and pops out a pill and gives it to me, I put it in my mouth, and then she holds out the glass of squash. Now they're singing in the living room. *Who can sail without the wind*, they sing. *Who can row without an oar*. I swallow. The squash is too strong. I give her back the glass and go into the hall and put my shoes on, Sonja following.

"Sweetie, where are you going?" she says.

"Out," I say.

I glance into the living room. It's just some darkness and some people. It's just a song. It's over now.

"Take care," I say.

"Take care," Dad says. "Take care, Robber's Daughter."

I go out into the corridor. It's bright. I have to shut my eyes, but I know what I'm going to do, and I can do it with my eyes shut.

But Aronsen doesn't answer. I knock and knock. Is it nighttime or something, why won't he open up? I can't bear the knocking sound, and the light in the corridor is strong, and we're not meant to look into the face of God, and I sit down with my back against his door and my head between my knees. No. I realise now what's happened. I realise now that Aronsen is dead. And that squirrel I saw once, that time we went on a class trip to the museum, and in the middle of the road, there it was, and there was blood and bursting guts, and we stopped walking, because the cars were driving over it, and the boys yelled, *more blood, more blood*, but not Meron. He stood next to me and understood, because death is death and all of us will die, even the yelling ones, so how can they yell, and Meron put his hands over my eyes. I get up and tug on the handle. It's locked. The handle is cold. Because Aronsen's not there. He's dead. And anyway, he's not my granddad, I don't even know where he is, I'm no one's grandchild and I don't even have his number, and now I know what's going on, Aronsen is dying in a house fire. Words can jinx, after all: I talked about a fire and now there's a fire, and Aronsen is burning to death, over and over, flinging himself against the window with the flames at his back, mothlike, open-mouthed and jinxed, cross my heart and hope to die, stick a fir needle in my eye.

But now the pill is starting to work. Yes.

It pours into my legs and arms and now. Now I'm off out for a bit.

All I have to do is follow my legs. They just walk, down the fire escape and out.

Here's the road. Here there's lights, here there's people and there's cars. It isn't night. It's only dark, people carrying plastic bags out of the supermarket, I've got to laugh. Lamps shine. Cars drive. And a voice calls, *Ronja, the man's turned red.*

Two angels come. One big and one small. It looks as though they're coming over here. But no, it's Musse. And far above is Musse's dad, see how nice they look, in angels' robes, and Musse with his denim jacket on top.

"It's the actual Musse," I say, but Musse doesn't smile back.

"Ronja, what's the matter with you?" he says. "You can't just walk out into the road, what's wrong with you, where are you going?"

"I'm off out for a bit," I say.

Musse stares at me.

"And you?" I say. "Where to next?"

"Just the mosque," Musse says.

I nod. I start to walk, but Musse's dad grabs my shoulders.

"You're not feeling well," he says.

"You speak Norwegian," I reply.

"Ronja," Musse says. "I think Dad's right. I don't think you're in the best shape right now."

Something beeps. Oh, I know what it is, it's the alarm on their phone. I know what that means, they've got to run.

"Time for prayers," I say. "Ready, set, *go*."

But they don't run. Musse's dad says something in their language. Musse takes off his jacket and holds it out. There's sheepskin inside. I stand still. Then his dad takes the jacket and pulls it over me and does up the buttons. Then Musse holds my hand and says, "Dad says we're going to take you home."

"No," I say.

I shake my head. My brain sloshes. Lamps shine. Hey, there's the lady-man and the dog, all dressed up with glitter round their necks.

"Dad?" Musse says. "She doesn't want to."

His dad is talking in long sentences now, and I don't understand the angel language they speak, just *Mustafa*, *Mustafa* every so often, but then Musse looks at me.

"Ronja, Dad says we have to take you to your family," he says. "We have to take you to Melissa or somebody."

"No," I say.

"Yes," says Musse.

"You won't be there in time for prayers," I say. "What prayers are you trying to be in time for?"

"Look, can you stop talking about prayers?" Musse says. "Dad's really stubborn, Ronja. He's not just going to let you wander off, okay?"

So we walk. We walk, all the way to Bethlehem, and at the market Musse lets go of my hand and carries on towards the shed, only there's no room at the inn there, but he doesn't know that. I sense his father behind me, sense a hand on each shoulder. Eriksen's floodlight beams across the trees. The stars are brightly shining. I have to smile.

"I used to work there," I say.

"Yes," says Musse's dad.

"Do you work?" I say.

"Yes," he says.

Two ladies carry a tree past us.

"Mountain fir," I say.

He doesn't say anything back. A gust of wind blows through my hair.

"We wait," says Musse's dad.

"Yes," I say. "We wait."

"Sister," says Musse's dad.

"Yes," I say. "Sister."

There she is, I see her. She's taking long strides. Musse runs alongside, they stop in front of us. Melissa wipes her forehead with her mitten.

"Hi," says Musse's dad. "She's unwell."

"I understand," Melissa says. "Thank you."

"Emergency room," says Musse's dad.

"I understand," Melissa says, holding out her hand towards me. "Thank you, you don't have to stay."

But Musse's dad doesn't let me go. He nods a lot and says *emergency room, emergency room*, he holds me with one hand and points with the other, and Melissa nods back and says *yes*, but then she takes a step forward and grabs my wrist, *thank you so much*, she says, *thank you so, so much* and *you take care now*, until at last Musse gets embarrassed and tugs at his dad's arm and says, *okay, let's go now, Dad*—and he lets me go.

Melissa pushes me in among the trees. She stops behind the mountain firs and takes off her mitten and feels my forehead.

"But what have you done?" she says. "What's the matter with you, why did you come here?"

"They brought me here," I say.

"But Ronja," she says, and her voice is funny.

"Or," I say. "I went off out for a bit."

"But," she says, "the shed is locked and you're all... like, what are we going to do? Where are you going to sit?"

I don't know. I shake my head, and Melissa looks up at the sky and whispers, *Jesus fuck. Little help would be nice*, and then she takes off her scarf and wraps it around my neck. The scarf is huge and red. I get tired, and I close my eyes.

When I open them again, Tommy is standing in front of me.

"See?" Melissa says.

"She's got to go to the emergency room," says Tommy. "I'll drive her."

"No," Melissa says.

"No?" says Tommy.

I close my eyes again, the little gust of wind blowing against my cheek. *Do you know what happens when people like us go to the emergency room?* Melissa says, *child services stick their oar in and everything*, and at first Tommy says nothing, then he says, *okay*, and then I'm being picked up. I'm lifted over Tommy's shoulder like a Christmas tree. He sets me down behind the shed and fetches a blanket and a camping stool.

"Here we go," he says, folding out the camping stool. "Sit yourself down here."

"But Tommy," says Melissa, "what if Eriksen comes?"

"What choice do we have?" says Tommy.

A moment passes. Then Melissa says, "I don't know."

Tommy puts the blanket around me. He says, *it'll all be fine, it's all right*, he pats me on the cheek, *I'll ring the missus*, he says, *her sister is a nurse*, but then he looks up, his head at an angle.

"Oh no," he says.

Then I hear what he hears. A big car with a big motor. A car door slamming. Tommy stands up and peers around the corner.

"It's Eriksen," he says.

Melissa puts her mitten to her mouth.

"Ronja, sit quietly," says Tommy. "Melissa, you go deal with the customers. I'll chat to Eriksen, try to keep him away."

He takes off his woolly hat. Leaning forward, he tugs it down onto my head.

"It'll all be fine, it's all right, ladybird," he says.

Then he drags Melissa off and they are gone.

"It's no use fighting," Dad likes to say. "Just forget it, the match is fixed."

And here I sit. I hear a lorry backing up, beeping. I hear Eriksen shouting, *yep*, he shouts, *bit more, bit more, stop*. I pull the hat down. It smells of Tommy. I pull the scarf up. It smells of Melissa. A boy runs past, he looks at me, but it's as though he doesn't see me. *Mum*, he shouts, *Mum, can I have a mini tree?*

Then there are no more customers, then there is only the wind.

It starts to rain, fast and hard. A newspaper blows past.

It's no use fighting. I take a breath. Whatever is to come, let it come. And now it comes.

Because now there are two shoes in front of me. And a voice says, "Well, well, well. Sitting back here, are we?"

It's a man. But it isn't Eriksen. It's someone else entirely.

He squats down. He holds out his hand towards me.

"Alfred," he says. "I'm a farmhand."

Alfred, I think. His hand is baking hot.

"I've heard about you," he says. "You know someone I know."

"Yes," I say. "The caretaker."

"Stick with me," says Alfred, standing up.

"I can't walk around very much," I say.

"With me, then," says Alfred.

He puts on gloves. There's a tree lying at his feet. He lifts it over his shoulder and reaches his free hand down to me.

"Hang on," he says.

My face is getting wet, it's raining straight at me. But Alfred puts me behind him, and I'm sheltered, and he's so broad it's like I'm walking behind a wall of rock. He stops under the floodlight. There he puts the tree down, and I see how tall it is, then he pulls the netting off, and I see how big it is.

"Is it a commercial-grade tree?" I say, but Alfred doesn't answer, only tilts the tree up and puts it in a free stand.

Then he turns to me and says, "It's yours."

"Mine?" I say.

"Your father said you wanted a tree," says Alfred. "I promised to hold on to this one."

He pats the branches. The needles are gleaming with rain.

"Finest fjord spruce in Enebakk," he says. "Don't sell it."

"I'm not selling anything," I say. "Child labour's not allowed."

"Good," says Alfred. "Because this tree isn't meant to be sold."

He takes off his gloves again. He places his hands on my cheeks. My whole head grows warm.

"It's meant for you to use," he says.

I shut my eyes. I nod.

"You take care," he says. "Ronja the Robber's Daughter."

Then he lets me go. I squeeze my eyes, I don't want to watch him leave. I hear the wind and the rain, and the door slamming, and the lorry starting up, now he's gone, and my face goes cold, and I'm freezing with the rain and wind. I open my eyes. He's gone, but the tree's still there.

It's still there. Swaying.

Its branches reach all the way to the ground. I glance around. Over by the shed, I see Eriksen unlocking the door. And quickly, like a squirrel, I slip in underneath the bottommost branches.

It's dry under here. That's how dense the needles of the finest fjord spruce are. Lifting a branch, I peep out. Receipts and biscuit wrappers and wisps of Christmas grain flutter across the tarmac. I've got to find Melissa, I've got to tell her where I am. But I can't see her, I can only see the shed, and a man with a dog who is running through the rain. The water splashes around his shoes.

Then the shed door opens. It's Eriksen. He looks around.

"Melissa!" Eriksen shouts. "Tommy!"

He's coming straight for me. But I guess he can't see me, because that's how dense the needles are on the finest fjord spruce. He stops in front of the tree, turns his back and shouts.

"Oy!" he shouts. "Come here!"

But look. Look what he's holding behind his back.

And here comes Melissa. Here comes Tommy. They know nothing. Melissa is twisting her mittens as she walks, Tommy picks a plastic bag up off the ground and puts it in his pocket. Then they're standing in front of me. With such open eyes.

"Well," says Eriksen. "I just had a little nose around the shed. And I found this notebook here."

"And you're telling me that girl's just here to do homework?" Eriksen says. "And you're telling me she has migraines and you're spinning tall tales and putting the blame on me?"

Nobody answers. The rain is like a curtain in front of them, sometimes thicker, sometimes thinner.

"Fraud," Eriksen says. "Fraud, big-time."

Then he holds up the notebook towards Tommy and says, "You two can forget about being paid for December."

"What?" says Tommy.

"Breach of contract," Eriksen says. "You're the one responsible here, and you're running a con? Classic breach of contract."

"No, please," says Tommy.

"What?" says Eriksen. "Please what?"

"It's only two weeks until the due date," Tommy says.

"Maybe you should have thought of that before

you scammed me," Eriksen says. "And you know what else? You've been engaging in child labour."

Melissa is just standing there, her mittens in her hands.

"That's a matter for the police," Eriksen says, nodding towards Tommy, then he points at Melissa and says, "and child services, as far as you're concerned."

Look. The wind is plucking at Tommy's scarf. It turns into a line, a long black line drawn by a felt-tip pen.

"Come with me to the shed," Eriksen says. "You can pack up your things."

I can't form a thought. I'm curling up inside my clothes. It's coming now, it's coming up from behind. I realise now that all of it is true, everything Dad likes to say, that we will die, and sandstorms and sicknesses will come, we will be scorched by sun in deserts, *we can't get out*, Dad says, *not out of our heads and not out of the world.* He's telling the truth, he really is, because everybody sits inside their own head and sees out of their own eyes, like cats in a crate, and now Eriksen is calling the police, and I know about prison, when Meron's brother came back out he was thin as a skeleton, even though he used to hang off the swings and lift his chin up to the bar a hundred times, and I know about child services, two ladies standing in the hall when we got back from the changing rooms, *hello, Emily*, they said, and Emily opened her mouth, and afterwards she walked away between them, we only saw her back, and her PE bag and wet hair, and later she wasn't around anymore. And what will Dad do, after that? Sit in

Stargate and gaze out into the dark. Wander round the flat without us, go into the corridor without us. Go down to the rubbish bins and not have anyone to throw out rubbish for.

And now I can't take anymore. Now I have to sleep.

So I lie down with my head on the tarmac and my back to the tree and fall asleep.

Summertime with Dad. When I came out of the sea and was shivering and Dad said, "Lie down on that black rock, Ronja. It's warmer."

And afterwards he found a piece of straw.

"Guess what I'm drawing now?" he said.

Then he drew on my back. And it was easy to guess, because he always drew the same thing: a sailboat.

Wintertime with Dad. When we carried the bags a long long way into the woods. And there we found the cabin, and he fastened the door with a hook and said that no one would be going out again that night, and anyway there was nothing outside, and anyway the buses had stopped running, and anyway there was no place else he'd rather be.

"Night night," Dad likes to say. "Sleep well, my Pearly Gates and my Shangri-La."

I'm woken by Melissa calling for me. I crawl out. Push aside a branch.

Everything is dark and wind-filled out here. Our sign has tipped over and the camping stool has flown in among the trees, and the trees, they're swaying this way and that. Melissa's pacing back and forth outside the shed and calling my name. Tommy stands on the pavement, his phone lit up in his hands. I crawl out and walk towards Melissa as the wind shoves me backwards, I have to push my legs forward one by one. I've never seen Tøyen like this. I put my hand on her back. She turns. First she stands still. Then she grabs me by the shoulders and begins to shake.

"You little shit!" she screams. "Where have you been?"

She shakes me and screams, *it's almost midnight*, she screams, *everything's gone fucked up since you went missing, I thought you'd frozen to death, I thought child services had got you*, and my head bounces back and forth, my hat falls off, *and we've searched all over Tøyen*, she screams, *what the hell are you playing at?* But in the end she stops shaking me. Then there's a gust of wind that slams into my ears and a tree topples and rolls towards us, stopping at our feet, and then there's silence.

"I just fell asleep under a spruce," I say.

"Huh?" Melissa says. "For hours? In this wind? How in the hell?"

"I don't know," I say, but then the wind picks up again, so she doesn't hear me.

She sinks to the ground. Then Tommy comes. He sits down next to her and puts his arm across her back. "She's here now, Melissa," he says.

She doesn't reply. Tommy hoists her up.

"Melissa, she's here now," he says. "You'd better go and talk to your dad."

But Melissa just hangs in his arms like a rag doll. Tommy looks at me.

"You've got to go home," he says. "Melissa has something she needs to explain to your dad. Melissa, you know what you're going to say, right?"

Melissa puts her arms around his neck. It's like she can't stand on her feet.

"Melissa, get it together," Tommy says, trying to loosen her grip, but she doesn't get it together. She gazes up at him.

Tommy looks around in all directions, but there's nothing there to help him, only rain, and wind, and an umbrella tumbling across the asphalt, the ribs sticking out at the sides. And me.

"Ronja," Tommy says. "When you see your dad, you've got to tell him child services are coming, and maybe the police as well."

"Okay," I say.

"And if he's ever going to stop drinking, now would be a good time," Tommy says.

I nod. Melissa crouches down again. Her coat is in a puddle. As she sits there rocking I can't see her face, only hair and arms. I go behind her and lift the coat. I hold it up like a bridesmaid.

"Okay," Tommy says. "Well, there's nothing more I can do."

"No," I say.

But he doesn't go. He stares at us.

"What is it?" I say.

"Nothing, I'm just wondering," says Tommy.

He blinks. He wipes his face with his sleeve.

"What's going to happen to you now?" he says.

Something flashes. I look up. The floodlight is hanging from its pole.

It's flashing at me.

And then I realise what we've got to do. I've been getting signs all along. It's just I didn't notice until now.

"Miracles do happen," the caretaker used to say. "Sometimes there just isn't any other way out, and that's when a miracle happens."

"Show that to your dad," the caretaker said.

And I stood there with the bit of paper in my hand, as the snow melted around it.

"Take care, Robber's Daughter," Dad said.

And I put on my shoes, I went.

"It's yours," said Alfred. "It's meant for you to use."

And so I crawled back underneath the tree.

And above it all there hung a star.

And now I'm standing here with Tommy and I understand everything, but he understands nothing, he's chewing his bottom lip.

"Tommy," I say.

"What?" he says.

"Don't be scared," I say. "Whatever happens next."

"Stop talking weird," he says. "You're really scaring me now."

I smile. He looks completely white.

"Take care, Tommy," I say. "You should be getting back to the missus."

I sit down next to Melissa. She glances up from underneath her hair. *There's no talking to Dad about this*, she says, *you know that, right*, and I say, *yeah, but please try to get up now*. She shakes her head, and her breaths are fast and strange. Tommy starts his car by the curb. The lights come on. Then it drives away. *And then in the middle of everything else I couldn't find you*, says Melissa, shaking and shaking her head, *it was like Judgment Day*, she says, *everything kind of slipping out of my hands, and maybe child services are with Dad right now, plus Tommy's losing his job, and what about his missus, what about the kid?*

But the floodlight's flashing up above. A thrill of hope.

"It's not a Judgement Day," I say. "It's Storm Gudrun."

She looks at me.

"Everything isn't slipping out of your hands," I say.

"Caramel, try to get up now," I say. "We can't just sit here in the middle of the storm."

I pull her up. Paper cups and big black plastic things are skittering across the ground. We walk, I'm holding her, we wade through pools of water, but I'm not scared anymore, and not sad anymore and not sick, because ahead of us the light is flashing, and I know where we have to go, but I don't think there's any way to say it. Then we're there.

"Look," I say. "This tree is from Dad."

Melissa doesn't say anything.

I lift up a branch. She just stands there.

"Finest fjord spruce in Enebakk," I say.

She shakes her head.

"Melissa, it's dry in there," I say. "Crawl underneath."

But she does nothing. I push her down and drag her in. Outside the rain is streaming on all sides, but here it's dry, it's like an island, it's as I knew it would be. I take off my jacket and lay it down with the sheepskin side up. Then I lift her arms and get her out of her coat.

"Look," I say. "Lie down here."

I nudge her down and lay her head on the jacket. I spread the coat over her. Then I sit down.

Once the storm is over, I think. But it doesn't sound like it will ever be over, it sounds like it's getting stronger and stronger.

Once morning comes, I think. I crawl forward and peep out. There's no morning coming yet. There's only this night now. The streetlamps sway and I see the rain in the light beneath them, the air striped with rain. And I'm not scared, but Melissa is, she's mewling like a cat.

"Shall I lie down with you for a bit?" I say.

She nods. I lie down behind her back. I pull the coat so it covers us. I can tell she's crying.

"Think of the woods," I say.

She doesn't answer.

"And a cabin in the woods," I say.

"But," she says.

"And a stove in the cabin," I say.

I put my mouth next to her ear. I tell her about the snow and the path.

Then you're walking up the hill.

   Then you see the fence.

   There you see the cabin. You see the light in the window.

She's sleeping now. I can tell it by her breathing. I lie down on my back. I close my eyes.

And when I wake, it's light.

"Melissa," I say. "We've got to go."

The sun makes stripes across her cheek.

"Melissa," I say. "You have to wake up."

She opens her eyes. Murk-eyes, puddle-eyes. She blinks and sits up.

I put the coat on her.

Then I push the branches aside.

"See?" I say. "It's our woods."

"See?" I say. "Now you get what I mean, don't you?"

I take her hand and drag her out, the snow sifting off the needles, glittering. Then I take a step forward, and above the trees the sky is bluer than blue, and the trees are whiter than white, and I take another step and everything gets brighter still, and look, over there's the squirrel, and yes, the trees are stooping like a portal.

"See?" I say. "There's our path."

Melissa nods.

"And you know where that goes, don't you?" I say.

"Yes," she says.

"Then let's go," I say. "All we have to do is go, Melissa."

That's how it ended.

It began and then it went on and in the end it ended. Yes. Seeds bud and become firs that sprout cones and grow and topple and die. People make up gods and forget them again, and still it all goes on. Seasons come and go, and behind the petrol station there will be no Christmas trees for sale now, only a few twigs on the ground, that's the circle of life. And every now and then there are days when the sun warms the sloping rock and you lie there on your belly. You dive into the sea and someone smiles at you below the waterline, but then you have to come up for air, that's how it goes. But not for us.

All we had to do was go, so we just went.

We held each other's hand. Melissa's coat dragged in the snow, she looked like a bride, only black. And it seemed as though the woods kept growing as we went, thickening around us, but the path was easy to walk, because the snow was trodden firm. Then there was a clearing, and we walked past the lake and up the hill where the fox has its den, and at the top you see a fence, and you'll follow that, and you know what you'll see then.

Yes, our clearing by morning. Sun shining over everything. And at evening. When the light is low and yellow through the tree trunks. When we knock the snow off on the doorstep. Then comes the dark.

Then we sit out on the step and watch the Big Dipper. And sometimes I think about Tøyen.

Then I think about Tommy. I hope everything's all right with the baby, and that he never has to work for Eriksen again, and I'm sorry for everything, I didn't mean for him to get all the blame. I think about the caretaker and hope things are going well with the spotlight and the home country, and I hope he knows I didn't mean that stuff about Norwegian, he's amazing at Norwegian, he could win the National Norwegian Championships. I think about Aronsen and hope someone grits the ground outside the flats properly, and that the wreaths last until New Year at least, and I think they will, because I chose the best.

And then I think about Dad.

I always do.

I lean my head against the doorframe. Then I dream, the way he taught me.

In the dream he's got the woolly jumper and his big smile. And in the dream he comes walking through the woods.

He knows the way, of course. Past the lake, up

the hill where the fox has its den. Then he sees the cabin, then he sees the step, then he sees us.

"Hello, girls," he might say then. "Is that the Diamond and the Emerald sitting there?"

And it gets so bright he has to put his sunglasses on.